Milo March is a hard-drinking, womanizing, wisecracking, James-Bondian character. He always comes out on top through a combination of personality, bluff, bravado, luck, skill, experience, and intellect. He is a shrewd judge of human character, a crack shot, and a deeper character than I have found in most of the other spy/thriller novels I've read. But, above all, he is a con-man—and a very good one. It is Milo March himself who makes the series worth reading.

—Don Miller, *The Mystery Nook* fanzine 12

Steeger Books is proud to reissue twenty-three vintage novels and stories by M.E. Chaber, whose Milo March Mysteries deliver mile-a-minute action and breezily readable entertainment for thriller buffs.

Milo is an Insurance Investigator who takes on the tough cases. Organized crime, grand theft, arson, suspicious disappearances, murders, and millions and millions of dollars—whatever it is, Milo is just the man for the job. Or even the only man for it.

During World War II, Milo was assigned to the OSS and later the CIA. Now in the Army Reserves, with the rank of Major, he is recalled for special jobs behind the Iron Curtain. As an agent, he chops necks, trusses men like chickens to steal their uniforms, shoots point blank at secret police—yet shows compassion to an agent from the other side.

Whatever Milo does, he knows how to do it right. When the work is completed, he returns to his favorite things: women, booze, and good food, more or less in that order....

D09889916

THE MILO MARCH MYSTERIES

The Twisted Trap
Six Milo March Stories

KENDELL FOSTER CROSSEN
Writing as
M.E. CHABER

With a Foreword by
KENDRA CROSSEN BURROUGHS

STEEGER BOOKS / **2021**

PUBLISHED BY STEEGER BOOKS
Visit steegerbooks.com for more books like this.

©2021 by Kendra Crossen Burroughs

First Edition

The unabridged stories have been lightly edited by Kendra Crossen Burroughs.

All rights reserved. No part of this book may be reproduced or utilized in any form or by any means, electronic or mechanical, without permission in writing from the publisher. The scanning, uploading, and distribution of this book via the Internet or via any other means without the permission of the publisher is illegal and punishable by law.

ISBN: 978-1-61827-585-1

CONTENTS

The Milo March Stories

Kendell Foster Crossen published more than sixty pieces of short fiction before deciding to write his first full-length novel. For that purpose he invented a new hero, named Milo March, a tough guy with a quick wit. "I wear a trench coat when it's raining. I carry a gun when somebody is trying to shoot me. I chase women, but only when they get that chase-me-look in their eyes." He has a seemingly unlimited capacity for booze. "Many people complain that I drink a lot. I do, but I also do the things that have to be done." There are two things that have to be done: "To solve the case I'm on and to stay alive."

Ken Crossen told an interviewer for a fanzine: "I worked out the character of Milo March, making him an insurance investigator since that was something I knew very well. I was to some degree influenced by Hemingway and Hammett, but added more of a dash of humor and more throwaway lines. Partly as a result of this, a later reviewer said that I wrote 'soft-boiled' novels." Milo March can be hard-boiled, yet he can also be gentle and compassionate. I fantasize that a lesson could be learned today from Milo's preference for shooting people without killing them. Could that be a holdover from Ken Crossen's pulp hero The Green Lama, a Buddhist who never carried a gun and would not kill, preferring more esoteric ways of disabling villains?

Milo made his debut in *Hangman's Harvest,* published in hardcover in February 1952. From there his exploits evolved into twenty more books, published between 1952 and 1973 under the pen name M.E. Chaber. The series acquired a following in the U.S. and abroad, but what really put Milo on the map was the mass-market series released by Paperback Library in 1970–1971, with the stylish, sexy cover art of Robert E. McGinnis.

Milo also appeared in nine pieces of short fiction published in magazines between 1952 and 1961. Three of them were condensed versions of full-length treatments: "Assignment: Red Berlin" is a shorter version of the novel *No Grave for March;* "The Man Inside" was expanded to become the novel of the same name; and "The Bodies Beautiful of Rome" is a condensed version of *A Lonely Walk.* Those three novels are in the present series, so the condensed versions are not included. That leaves the six short stories that are brought together in this volume.

Although the character was intended to be an insurance investigator, Milo was also in the Army during World War II and is still an officer in the Reserves. So in some of the books Major March is recalled to carry out dangerous missions for the CIA.

Oddly, Milo performs neither of these roles in the first book. In *Hangman's Harvest* he's just a plain private eye, on loan from a Denver insurance firm to clean up a vice-ridden California town. The next book in the series is a spy novel, *No Grave for March*, in which our hero is sent to East Germany. So Milo doesn't actually tackle an insurance case until the first short story. "The Jelly Roll Heist" (1952) and two other stories (1953) are centered on jewel robberies, each with its own twists and surprises.

Another oddity is that even though Milo is a resident of Denver (until he moves to New York City in 1956), none of the first five novels is set there, since Milo is always traveling to other cities and countries. So only in three of the short stories does the action take place in the Mile High City.

By 1961, the publication date of the last two stories, Milo has set up his own insurance detective agency in New York City, with an office on Madison Avenue. But almost as soon as the story "The Red, Red Flowers" begins, he is summoned from the martini capital, is flown over Soviet Russia, and parachutes in, just outside Moscow. A few of the elements in "The Red, Red Flowers" are also present in two novels set in Russia—*So Dead the Rose* (1959) and *Wild Nights in Moscow* (1968). It's not uncommon for a writer to recycle material or rework details from one story to another. What does strike me (though I don't want to give anything away) is that in "The Red, Red Flowers" Crossen seems to have seized the opportunity to create a happier outcome, as if he wanted to go back and set things right.

The title story, "The Twisted Trap," revisits, in a different context, the horrible predicament central to the plot of *The Splintered Man* (1955), in which a man is being dosed, without his knowledge, with a drug that causes schizophrenia-like symptoms such as hallucinations and distorted thinking—LSD. Crossen also explored LSD in a young adult novel, *The Acid Nightmare* (1967), in which a teenager experiences a good trip and then a bad trip. It's interesting that Crossen was fascinated by LSD, yet he himself had never taken it, relying on research to write the accounts of trips. I showed the passages from *The Splintered Man* to a professional expert, who confirmed that the descriptions of LSD experiences are credible.

Over the course of a prolific career, Ken Crossen created many detective characters, including a book reviewer, a playwright, a crime reporter, a few police detectives, a mortician, and a Buddhist monk—in addition to insurance investigators,* and even an intergalactic investigator in the humorous Manning Draco science fiction stories. The insurance investigator was a natural choice, since Ken himself had worked in that business as a young man in Ohio. But Milo March was special, becoming the author's favorite of all the sleuths whose stories he published under five pseudonyms. So strong was the identification with that personality that Crossen would tell a columnist in the *Los Angeles Times:* "Milo March is simply myself."

Kendra Crossen Burroughs

---

* Two other such characters (who appeared in *Detective Fiction Weekly* in 1940 and 1941) were Paul Anthony in "Homicide on the Hook" and Johnny "Mad" Hatter in "The Cat and the Foil," "The Ears of Loretta," "The Miniature Murders," and "Trouble with Twins." Beginning in 1956, under the pseudonym Christopher Monig, Crossen also wrote four novels about an insurance investigator named Brian Brett, which appeared in the Paperback Library series as well.

Milo March Short Fiction by M.E. Chaber

"The Jelly Roll Heist." *Popular Detective,* September 1952 (vol. 43, no. 2).

"Assignment: Red Berlin." *Bluebook,* December 1952 (vol. 96, no. 2).

"Hair the Color of Blood." *Bluebook,* July 1953 (vol. 97, no. 3).

"The Hot Ice Blues." *Bluebook,* September 1953 (vol. 97, no. 5).

"Murder for Madame." *Popular Detective,* Fall 1953 (vol. 45, no 1).

"The Man Inside." *Bluebook,* December 1953 (vol. 98, no. 2).

"The Bodies Beautiful of Rome." *Cavalier,* July 1957 (vol. 5, no. 49).

"The Red, Red Flowers." *Bluebook,* February 1961 (vol. 100, no. 3).

"The Twisted Trap." *Bluebook,* June 1961 (vol. 100, no. 5).

1

The Jelly Roll Heist

The Inter-World Insurance Service Corporation is in the Gilmore Building in Denver. Tenth floor. Three private offices and a reception room. At the outside desk there is a receptionist. Peaches-and-cream skin and blue-black hair; built-in accessories that have made many a man forget why he came up the ten stories. The door behind her has frosted glass and small black letters that say *Milo March.* That's all. Nothing to indicate that I was on the other side of the door and that I'd been there since nine in the morning, wading through reports, mostly my own, until I had diamonds in my eyes.

It was almost time to quit for the day when my phone rang. It was the peaches-and-cream skin and the blue-black hair. "You still sober, Milo?" she wanted to know.

After thinking it over, I decided to be insulted. On my desk there were two ounces of brandy that I'd been nursing since four o'clock, and there was still one sip left.

"Take your trade elsewhere, girl," I said with dignity. "I'm too busy to see you tonight." Which was a laugh. Our receptionist was a strictly-for-keeps girl. I knew. I'd tried enough times.

She laughed. "He wants to see you," she said. "Now."

I hung up and finished the brandy. "He" was Niels Bancroft, the owner and president of Inter-World. A nice guy. He never bothered me when I was working on a job, and he knew that for two weeks I'd been digging in. Somebody was working my side of the street. In six months, there had been almost a million dollars' worth of jewelry lifted in Denver or near it. All of it from women. The individual jobs had run from $10,000, the smallest, to $150,000 in diamonds. The insurance companies were screaming, and the whole thing was my baby. So if Niels wanted to see me, it meant that there was a new case to add to the others or that the insurance companies were getting hotter.

I walked out of my office and turned to the middle door. It was solid oak, as simple looking as a thousand-dollar bill, with Niels's name on it in the kind of letters that made it unnecessary to read further to know that it also said *President* and *Private*. I opened the door and stepped inside.

Niels Bancroft is a big man who looks like an ex-pug. His hair is gray and there are little gray tufts sticking out of his ears. He's a chain smoker and sticks half a cigarette in his mouth. He wears $200 suits and a $500 watch, but he still lights my cigarettes with big kitchen matches. He looked up as I came in and motioned me to a chair.

"How's it going, Milo?" he asked.

"You just asking or you want to know?" I said. "If it's the first—fine. If it's the second—how much time do you have?"

Niels grinned at me. We'd worked together a long time and understood each other. "I want to know," he said. "Not all of it. Just give me a couple of high spots. You sound annoyed, so you must be getting somewhere."

"Yes and no." I lit a cigarette. "I talked to Selsden on the Robbery Squad first. They have so little that they might as well have left the reports on the squeal books. They think these were all one-man jobs and that all the victims were involved, because every one of them had a shaky story. Beyond that, they're still beating the woods."

"But you're not?"

"I'm a city boy myself," I said. "They're right about the shaky stories. I talked to every woman involved, and it was plain they were all concealing something. I worked on one of them and found out why." I grinned at him.

"Why?"

"She had a boyfriend. For a few days before the robbery and for a few days after it. Then he left. Part of her shaky story was that she came home, alone, from a party and left the sparklers on the dressing table in her bedroom. But she never heard any burglars. You know why? For thirty minutes she and the boyfriend were in the bathroom taking a shower together, just like two innocent kids. With variations, you can bet the same thing happened in the other cases."

"Description?"

"One that wouldn't fit any more than maybe a hundred thousand guys. Even a better description wouldn't buy us much. You can also bet that most of these women, maybe all of them, aren't going to make any identification downtown."

"Why not?" he demanded.

"You're not thinking, Niels. I've told you how the jobs were pulled. A pretty guy. A lot of romance. When the stage is set, the pretty boy leaves the door unlocked, takes the babe to the shower or a Simmons version of the haystack, while his friend walks in and out. All of them. Even old Mrs. Russel, who's having her change-of-life fling. Most of them are married. None of them want a court reporter taking down such details."

"No other leads to the guy?"

"I know who he is," I said. "Remember a guy the newspapers called the Romantic Burglar? A few years ago."

He nodded. "Vander, or something like that. He was sent up, wasn't he?"

"But he's been out a year. He's in and around Denver. He always had a liking for jewelry. He used to work alone."

"Teamed up?"

I nodded. "Something like that. I got a few odd pieces of information out of Whistles Naylor. He sings a pretty tune if you're nice to him. He doesn't know the pitch on this, but he does know that Willie Vander is around town and that he's been moving in the upper social circles occasionally. When he's not, he stays at that new sanatorium just out of town."

That made his eyebrows go up. "Big-time stuff," he said.

"Dr. Lewis Mora's private sanatorium," I said. "The doctor being better known as Lew Mora, on the payroll of Joe Rinchetti.* Joe has been out here for his health ever since the Kefauver Committee was playing the circuit.** There are other

---

* A mobster in the sanatorium business is not too far-fetched. Colorado's climate and elevations made it a haven for tuberculosis patients, and its many sanatoriums (some of them luxurious spas) helped to enrich the state. By the time this story was published, antibiotics had already become a more effective TB treatment than fresh air, and sanatoriums were eventually transformed into hospitals. (All footnotes were added by the editor.)
** The Special Committee on Organized Crime in Interstate Commerce (1950–1951) was a five-member committee initially chaired by Senator Estes Kefauver. The television broadcasts of its hearings made the Kefauver Committee a household term.

assorted buck hustlers out there, too. My guess is they're keeping their hand in, making cigarette money and grooming Vander as their steady boy."

"You got proof?" he asked.

"Nothing that a judge would want to hear," I said. "All I can do is keep digging. Maybe I'll catch him the next time out."

"He's already been out again," Niels said sourly. "You ever hear of Ylla Hamal?"

I shook my head. "I missed *Pogo* this morning. Must be somebody new in Okefenokee."

"Funny," he said flatly. "Ylla Hamal is a Turkish dancer. A belly dancer, she's called. She's taken America by storm. Forty-nine weeks on Broadway. On her third week in Denver. At a place called Little Egypt."

"That's the way it goes," I said. "Burlesque is out, belly dancers are in. You've got to pay a cover charge if you want to be exposed to immoral influences. I know the Little Egypt. It's on the slumming circle for the upper fry."

"That's it," Niels said. "She was robbed last night. A ten-carat ruby. Fifteen thousand dollars' worth of insurance. You go out and see her at the club tonight."

"Why tonight?"

"She likes to sleep in the daytime, and I hear she's also in a hurry." He grinned. "She wore that ruby in her navel. I guess she's practically naked without it. Anyway, you run out and examine the scene of the crime." He built the grin up to a chuckle.

"Funny," I said in the same tone of voice he'd used earlier. I stood up and looked at him, "Belly dancers and navel tiaras.

Someday I'm going to walk out of here and buy myself a chicken farm."

"You wouldn't know which end of the chicken to milk," he said. "Run along now. You're in charge of our navel operations."

There was only one way to keep him from building a whole act out of it. I closed the door behind me as I stepped into the reception room. I could still hear him laughing.

"What's with him?" our receptionist asked, looking up. "Did you ask him for a raise, or some such pleasantry?"

"He just cut himself on an old joke," I said. "You might go in and pour a little iodine over him later. ... Take a look and see if we have any pictures of Willie Vander."

She got up and walked over to the filing cabinets. They were disguised to look like some sort of console. Even if I hadn't wanted the picture, it would have been worth asking for it just to watch her walk.

After a bit she came back with a picture. It was a five by seven, so I could carry it without cracking the gloss. It was maybe five years old, but that was close enough. He was a good-looking guy, all right.

"Working tonight, Milo?"

"Yeah," I said. "A belly dancer lost her family jewels."

"Belly dancer?" She dimpled at me. "That ought to be about your speed."

"What do you know about speed?" I said. "You're always parked." I left before she could think up an answer.

I went home and changed clothes and shaved, had a couple of

drinks, and went out to dinner. Finally, around nine o'clock, I drove down to the Little Egypt.

It was like a thousand other nightclubs scattered throughout America. A small room with a circular bar, then a larger room with the tables almost against each other. There were only a few people in the club when I got there. An orchestra was playing Cuban music.

The headwaiter was on his toes. He met me halfway through the door, and you could tell that he'd already figured out how much my suit cost and which pocket I carried my money in. He got off his toes as soon as I told him what I wanted. He told me that Miss Hamal had not yet arrived at the club. He would tell her as soon as she did arrive. His manner suggested that it might be a good idea if I waited in the men's room, but I went to the bar.

I had a couple of brandies. At the price, there should have been a ten-carat ruby in each drink. But it was expense account drinking, so I tossed it off as if I always paid a buck an ounce for my brandy.

I'd just finished the second drink when the headwaiter came back and indicated that I could follow him if I had nothing better to do. We skirted the main room and went backstage, where it looked as if someone was thinking of opening a line of closets. He pointed to a door and went tripping back to his chores.

I went over and knocked on the door. *"Giriniz,"* a voice called through the door. I opened the door and stepped inside. The dressing room was about the size and shape of a cracker box with delusions of grandeur, but I didn't have much chance to look it over. She'd been sitting at a dressing table, but when I entered, she stood up and held out her hand.

I didn't see her hand at first. She was tall, maybe five eight. Long black hair. Black eyes, the kind that seem to have lights in them. Her figure was all curves, every one of them nice. Dark, creamy skin. Lots of it—she was already in her costume. A strip of net over her breasts, with two little silver crescents the only part that wasn't transparent. There was a beaded string around her waist, and just below it was a slightly larger silver crescent. That was her costume. It didn't leave anything to the imagination, but after one look at her, you didn't care if you ever imagined.

"Nasılsınız?" she said. "You are from the insurance company, no?" It was a pleasant accent.

I managed to get my gaze back up to her face, and I could tell that she knew it had been a strain. A little smile was tugging at the corners of her full mouth.

"I am from the insurance company, yes," I said. "I'm Milo March.

"I'm glad," she said. I wasn't sure whether she was glad I was Milo March or that I was from the insurance company. "You will forgive the costume, please? It is that I have to dance soon, but I wish to tell you about the robbery too."

"I'll forgive the costume," I said, taking another look at it. Then grinned. *"Bana bir ufak i e kanyak ve taze çay getir- iniz."* I managed a little chuckle.

She laughed. It was a nice laugh.

"You liked that, huh?" I said, pleased with myself.

She nodded. "Very amusing."

"I must be improving," I said. "That's the first time I ever got a laugh by saying 'Bring me a small flask of brandy and some fresh tea' in any language. It must be my delivery."

We stared at each other while she thought that one over. Then she laughed again. This time it was an even nicer laugh.

"Okay," she said. "It used to be Sally Moore of Brooklyn before I changed it to Ylla Hamal. But who wants to see a Brooklyn girl do the belly dance? Was that the McCoy you spoke?"

"Yeah," I said. "I was over there during the war. That was out of the book the Army gave me. It told you how to ask for everything but what the G.I. really wanted. Now that we have Brooklyn and Turkey straightened out, what about the ruby?"

"I really feel naked without it," she said, patting her stomach. I didn't point out that maybe she felt that way was because she was. "I met this guy the second week I was here. He said his name was Bob Williams, but I don't think it was. He came around every night, and I have to admit I went for him a little. He was plenty good-looking and seemed to have money. Then, last night, he came around between the first and second shows. Later, he said he had to run home but he'd be down by the last show. After he was gone, I discovered the ruby was gone, too." There was a wry smile on her face. You could see she didn't like being taken.

"Okay," I said. I gave her a cigarette and took one myself. I lit both of them. "You always just toss the ruby on the dressing room table or something in between acts?"

She gave me a long look from beneath her lashes. "I'm going to level with you, Milo," she said slowly. "If I can't get my ruby back, I want the insurance. But I'd rather have the ruby than the money. I didn't tell the cops the whole story. No reason, except I don't like cops."

I nodded. I had a hunch that she was going to be the one who'd give us the identification. She acted as if she was mad enough.

"This guy," she said, "was throwing passes from the first. Without getting to first base. But as I said, I was beginning to go for him. I guess I was feeling a little romantic last night. ... I don't know when he copped the ruby."

"Where was it?"

"Where do you think?" she said. She rubbed one hand across her stomach. "Once I put the ruby on, it stays there until the last show. It's cemented in. It doesn't come off easy,"

I nodded, suppressing a grin. It looked as if Willie had decided he'd show the gang he could pull at least one job strictly on his own. Just to make sure, I fished the picture from my pocket and showed it to her.

"That's him," she said. "He's got a record, huh?"

"One of the long-playing ones," I said. "With some help, he's pulled three dozen jobs in the past six months around here. All of them women."

She mentioned a few thoughts she had about Willie's personal habits and his immediate ancestry.

"Now," I said, "if he's pulled in, will you identify him? This is the big problem. I don't think anyone else will identify him."

"Look, Buster," she said, and her voice was suddenly harsh, "I didn't get that ruby from an itchy John. I bought it with my own dough. The hard way. Bumps and grinds on the runway.

As far as the act's concerned, I can get along well with the piece of red glass I'm going to use tonight. But I want that ruby back. You find the guy, and I'll canary all over the place."

"Okay, honey," I said. I reached for the door and took a last look at her costume, just to show that I was still fashion-minded. "I'll see you around."

"Why don't you stay and catch the show?" she asked. Her voice was soft again. "I'm good."

"I'm sure you are," I said, "but I'm not sure that my blood pressure could stand it. Maybe after this is over."

I went out and found my way back to the bar, where I treated myself to a couple more brandies on the insurance companies and thought it over. This might blow the case open. If I wanted to go easy on myself, I could tip off the robbery detail, let them pick up Willie, Ylla would provide the identification, and that would be it. But I never like to have cops do my work for me. Maybe I'd push around a little first and see if something fell. I went out and climbed into my old car and headed downtown.

Whistles Naylor was a little character who'd been on the stuff a long time. A needle man. Once in a while he'd pull a purse-snatch or a small heist. That, and what he picked up for singing, kept him going. I don't think anyone knew his first name. He'd been called Whistles for years because he'd blow the whistle on anybody if the price was right, and almost everyone knew it. In spite of this, he still managed to pick up information. He lived in a broken-down rooming house, and I figured that he'd still be in his room. Whistles's day didn't start until pretty late at night.

I parked the car around the corner. The front door of the house was never locked, so I went up the dark stairs. The house smelled of onions, cheap whiskey, and dirt. I knocked on his door. There was a moment of silence, then I heard a scurrying sound inside. More silence.

"Yeah?" he said through the door. His voice was high and nervous.

"Milo March," I said.

He opened the door enough to look out, then wide enough for me to slip in. The room was lit by a weak blue bulb, which didn't make Whistles look any prettier. Probably nothing would have helped. He was a little ratty-looking character with a twitchy face. There were only two things in his life—a hunger for heroin and the fear that he might tell too much sometime.

He blinked at me in the dim light. "Whatsa matter, Milo?" he asked. He was just nervous enough to tip that he was getting to the point of needing a shot. If he hadn't already taken it, it was because he was broke.

"I want some more on Willie Vander," I said.

"But I already told ya everything I know," he said. "I wouldn't hold out on ya, Milo, I need the dough too much. Jeez, if I only had a sawbuck—"

"You can earn it," I interrupted. "I want the last-minute dope on Willie. Tonight. I want to know if he's still at the sanatorium and if he's going to stay there. I want to know who else is with him. I want to know if they've fenced any of the hot jewelry yet."

"Ya know I'd do it if I could, Milo," he whined, "but, jeez, sometimes I can pick up things and sometimes I can't. If I go asking, they'd bump me sure. You know that, Milo."

I looked at him. I figured that Whistles ought to have the chance for one little fling. He deserved that much, at least.

"Whistles," I said, "if you can get what I want in the next hour or so, I'll give you three thousand dollars. You can get away on that and still have enough for plenty of needles."

"Three grand," he said. His hands were shaking. "Maybe I can do it, Milo. But I'll need a few bucks to get into a place."

I took out five dollars. "I don't want you getting high first, Whistles," I said, "but here's five bucks. The minute you get the dope, I'll give you enough for a needle. And three grand in the morning." I handed him the bill. He tucked it away with a furtive gesture. "In one hour back here," I said.

He nodded, and I left the room. Downstairs, I waited in a dark place in the hallway. When Whistles came down, I followed him. I knew he hadn't been kidding when he said he might be killed for trying to get me the information. I didn't want that on my conscience, too, so I was going to trail along.

We went across town, and after fifteen blocks or so, Whistles ducked into a bar. I waited about five minutes before going in after him.

It was like a dozen other holes. There were three or four tables and a long bar. It looked as though there might be rooms in the back, and I was sure of it when I realized that Whistles wasn't anywhere in sight. There were two bartenders and a waiter, all three obviously of the brotherhood of thugs. About half the customers in the place were just customers; the other half had probably never done anything more strenuous than hefting a blackjack or holding a .38. I stood at the bar and ordered a brandy.

It was forty-five minutes and four brandies later when I saw Whistles. He came out of the back. There were two men with him. Both were dressed well, with the kinds of jackets that are cut to hide a bulge under the left arm. Whistles looked pretty unhappy. One of the men stopped at an empty table, and the other went into the men's room with Whistles. The waiter didn't bother to go near the table.

I finished a drink and nodded to the bartender to fill it up again. Leaving my change on the bar, I walked casually in the direction of the men's room. Practically no one was paying any attention to me, but I could feel a slow tightening in the atmosphere.

I was almost to the door when the man at the table got up and stepped in front of me.

"Where you going, chum?" he asked.

I looked at him as if he wasn't quite in focus and gestured at the door.

"Uh-uh," he said. "There's somebody in there what likes privacy. You buy yourself another drink and come back later."

"You know how it is," I said. I gave him a foolish grin and edged a little closer. "When you gotta go, you gotta go. You let me go in and then I'll buy both of us a drink. Huh?" I threw one arm around his shoulder and blew some brandy in his face.

"Take a powder," he grunted, and tried to throw my arm off.

I wrestled him around until my back was to the bar. Then

I reached in and pulled the .38 from my shoulder holster. I snapped the barrel up against the point of his jaw. It made a solid, satisfying sound. I caught him as he sagged. Then, as if it were still a game, I waltzed him over to the table and lowered him in the chair. I let his head rest on the table and looked around. The waiter was watching me. He started to move forward.

I twisted my body just enough, holding the gun close to my stomach. The edge of my coat hid it from the rest of the room, but the waiter could see it, all right. It was pointed at him, and he stopped, his eyes respectful.

"Some people don't know when they've had enough to drink," I said to him. "Better let him sleep it off."

"I guess you're right," he said carefully. He was still watching my gun.

"I'll still have it when I come out," I said. "Why don't you go wash a few dishes or order yourself a sandwich?"

I waited until he had shuffled off into the kitchen, then turned and went into the men's room. Whistles Naylor was on the floor, and a trickle of blood was coming from one corner of his mouth. The other guy stood over him, leaning down, ready to punch again. I saw a glint of metal on his fist. He looked at me without really seeing me.

"Beat it, chump," he said. "This is private."

"So is this," I said.

This time he saw the gun, and his whole body stiffened. He straightened up slowly, being careful not to make any sudden move.

"Who are you?" he asked flatly.

"Milo March," I said. He didn't seem to know my name. "I usually help old ladies across the street, but I guess this'll do as a good deed. On your way, friend. Outside."

He started to walk stiff-legged past me toward the door. As he reached me, I shifted the gun to my left hand and hit him right where his jaw hinged. He did a running stagger into one of the cubicles, sat on the seat for a minute, then slid to the floor. He was on ice for a while. I slipped the gun back in its holster and turned to Whistles.

"Come on," I said.

He scrambled to his feet. His face was so white it made the blood look twice as bright. "They'll kill us, Milo," he said. He was shaking all over.

"Not until they come to, at least," I said. "Let's get out of here."

This time he followed me. We went out into the bar, past the hood who was still slumped over the table. Some of the conversation was still going on, but there were a handful of men who weren't saying anything. Their silence followed us right out onto the sidewalk.

"Can you get it near here?" I asked Whistles. I knew he wouldn't be any good now until he'd had a shot.

"Yeah," he said through chattering teeth. "About three blocks from here."

"How much?"

"Double sawbuck."

I gave him twenty dollars, and we walked down the street. I waited near an alley while he went into a ramshackle apartment building. He was back in about fifteen minutes, and we walked across town again. By the time we reached my car, he was feeling no pain.

"Did you get anything?" I asked when we were seated in the car.

"I'll say I did," he said. He was sounding brave now. "Willie is staying at the doctor's joint out of town, all right. Just like I told you. There's some big shots there from the East, and all of them are tied in with Manny Dane here in town. They're riding high, and Willie's going to pull another job tomorrow night."

"Where?"

"A joint called the Groove Grove. One of Manny's guys hangs around there all the time. Reet Coles. Maybe you know of him. Anyway, they got a babe coming there tomorrow night—a singer. She wears a lot of rocks, and Reet is going to arrange for Willie to meet her. Hack Willer—one of the guys back there—is gonna cover him."

I nodded. I knew the Groove Grove. It was a hot jazz outfit that drew a mixed crowd. Not only black and tan, but everything from uptown class to the weed addicts.

"What's the singer's name?"

He shook his head. "Didn't get it."

"What about the jewelry? Have they fenced any of it?"

"They said something about going to make a deal. But I didn't hear any more. That was when Hack threw the door open and found me listening. Milo, you won't forget you promised?"

"You'll get it," I said. "Now we're going to find you another room. You stay in it and I'll bring you the money in the morning,"

A few blocks away, we found a vacancy in another crummy rooming house. I took the room myself under a phony name and then took Whistles quietly up the stairs. He'd be safe as long as he stayed put.

I'd had some idea of going out to the sanatorium, but what Whistles had told me gave me another idea. So I went home to bed.

I was up early the next morning and in the office a few minutes before Niels. By the time he arrived, I'd typed out my little sheet of paper and was waiting for him.

"My expense account for last night," I told him as I handed it to him. He glanced at it, and sudden red spots showed on his cheeks. "What the hell's this?" he demanded. "Three thousand dollars for entertainment. You buy somebody a mink coat on the expense account?"

"I listened to a song," I said. "I promised the guy three thousand, and it was worth it."

"The insurance companies won't like it, Milo."

"You think they'd like it better if I gave them a breakdown?" I asked. "You think maybe they'd like to know how many ounces of heroin their money's going to pay for?"

Shaking his head, he said, "There's another angle. Great Northern in New York called me at home before I left this morning. They covered most of the jewelry that's been lifted. I think their share runs a little more than seven hundred thousand. Well, they've been approached about a deal. They can have everything back for two hundred thousand. They wanted to know what they should do."

"What did you tell them?"

"I said I'd call them back after I'd talked to you."

"Okay," I said. "Call them back and tell them they owe us three thousand dollars. If they pay us the three grand and give us forty-eight hours, maybe they'll have their stones. But I want the three grand now."

He grumbled some more, then went over to a small safe, took out the money in small bills, and handed it over. I was just going out when our girl said there was a phone call for me. I took it at the reception desk.

"Milo?" said a man's voice. "This is Murray Malikoff, in case you've forgotten." I hadn't forgotten. He was a lieutenant in Homicide, a good cop.

"Hi, Murray," I said. "How are things in the baser passions department?"

"Still knocking 'em dead," he said. "Milo, I hear you're looking for a guy named Willie Vander. Used to be the Romantic Burglar."

"Where'd you hear that?"

"Oh, once in a while someone tells the cops something. Not often. Is it true?"

"I was looking for him," I said. "But now I know where to find him."

"Sure," he said. "In the morgue."

I should've seen it coming, but I hadn't. "I'll come over later and tell you about it."

"That's a very good idea," he said softly. "Willie was killed with a .38. Then we had a call from someone who said you'd been looking for him and that maybe you'd caught up with him. So you come over and tell us all about it. It would be a real favor."

I swore. "You ought to know better than that, Murray."

"I don't know anything," he said. "I just like to have people confide in the police. So you come over."

I figured quickly. "Give me an hour," I said.

"I'll be here," he said. "So will Willie."

I put the receiver back on the hook and got out quick. I'd started worrying about Whistles as soon as Murray told me about Willie, but as I drove downtown I convinced myself that he was probably all right.

My friend Whistles was right where I'd left him. He was beginning to worry about me, too, but for different reasons. I took him out to breakfast, but he only nibbled at it. Then I let him buy himself a shot and a spare. After that I took him to the airport and bought him a ticket on the first plane out in any direction. I slipped the rest of the money to him just as he went through the gate. Then I drove back to Homicide as quickly as I could. Malikoff was in his office.

"You might as well start by checking this," I said. I took out my gun and put it on the desk. "Then you won't go around wondering if you missed something. When did you find Willie?"

He called a detective in and handed my gun to him. Then he turned back to me. "One block away on the street. Real convenient. Doc says he was killed early this morning and carried here. Two shots through the head."

I told him the whole story, leaving out only what Ylla Hamal had failed to tell the police. I also kept out the amount of payment to Whistles and the fact that he'd already left town. It wouldn't help to solve the case, and I felt that Whistles deserved his fling in peace.

"I think it adds up like this," I concluded. "Willie was working with some local boys and the Eastern gang out at the sanatorium, but Willie was the only one out front. He was the only one who could be identified, and they thought they had that sewed up. But after they caught Whistles eavesdropping and I came to the rescue so fast, they must have decided it was later than they knew. They think they're about to make a deal with the insurance company, and it might have been embarrassing if Willie was pulled in. So they canceled him out. The call about me was probably just an idea on the part of one of those two guys last night."

"Hack Willer, huh?" he said. "I've met him, but maybe I ought to meet him again."

The detective came back in with my gun, He shook his head slightly as he put it on the lieutenant's desk. I picked it up and slid it back into the holster.

"I don't think it'll get you anywhere fast," I said. "From their point of view, this has been a small operation so far, but they're big operators. Don't make any mistake about that."

"I won't," he said. He looked at me in a half-friendly fashion. "Don't you make any mistakes either, Milo."

I grinned and left him.

At first glance, it had seemed that the killing of Willie Vander had washed up the idea I had. I thought about it a while and decided maybe it would still work, with variations.

It didn't take long to find out about the singer who was opening at the Groove Grove. Her name was Geri Stack. She was a blues singer. Not the pops kind, but the real New Orleans article. In fact, practically the only white singer to hit those genuine dirty notes. I checked with the office and found she had jewelry worth about thirty thousand. She wore most of it when she sang.

I checked around some more and found she'd already arrived in Denver and was staying at the Hotel Wallander. I even got a list of the places where she was supposed to be during the day. The best bet looked like the Dixie Record Shop. She was to be there from eleven to eleven-thirty.

When I was younger, I'd gone through a period of being strictly a Dixie character. I still liked jazz, although it didn't give me the kind of send-off it once had. But I still had everything I'd bought in those days. I went back to my apartment and scrounged around among the records. As I'd thought, a number of them were probably collectors' items now. After a while, I picked on a very early Armstrong, from the days when he had his first small combo. Considering the use I was going to make of it, I thought even Satchmo would approve the sacrifice.

I killed a little time with some brandy and then went downtown, stopping in at a newspaper morgue to get a look at a photograph of Geri Stack. When I saw it, my interest in my work picked up. By eleven-fifteen, I was outside the record shop with the Armstrong tucked under my arm.

I caught a glimpse of her just as she was about to leave. I timed myself just right, so that when she had swung the door out, it caught me on the shoulder. I spun around, and the big glass window kept me from falling. I'd lost the record at the beginning of the spin and had managed to step on it once, to make sure.

"Oh, I'm sorry," she said. It was a nice voice, but I didn't look up. I just stood there, starring down at the broken record, I hoped I looked broken-hearted. Finally, she bent down to look, too.

" 'St. Louis Blues,' " she said. She bent lower and took a better look. "Satchmo's first platter of it. Oh, I'm terribly sorry. Please let me pay you for it."

"I wasn't going to sell it," I said. This time I looked at her as if she were just another dame who'd busted a record.

She knew the value of the record, not just in dollars and cents but in other coin. We were already related by shattered wax. "There must be something I can do to show you how I feel," she said.

This time I let myself see her. "Say," I said, "you're Geri Stack, aren't you?"

She nodded. You could see she liked being Geri Stack—in a nice way.

"Then maybe you'd—" I broke off and shook my head. "I'm sorry, Miss Stack. That would be taking advantage of you."

She gave me a smile. "Come on," she said. "We're just a couple of cats standing over a broken trumpet note. Don't be a square."

I gave her a little bit of man-looking-at-a-woman, then went back to being a cat. "I was going to ask you to have lunch with me," I said. "That would be worth a lot of acetate."

She frowned and looked at her watch. I held my breath. My idea involved her, but my hunch was that if I suggested it cold, she'd say no. So I had to hope this would work. I think she was about to refuse when her gaze caught the broken record again.

"All right," she said suddenly. "I've got an hour and a half. It's a small enough price to pay for an Armstrong. Where'll we go?"

"The Hickory House," I said. I took her arm, and we started looking for a cab while a gang of fans watched us through the store windows. "And the name is Milo March, Miss Stack."

We found a taxi and went to the Hickory House. Good food and a sense of privacy. Any way I looked at it, I was pleased. The first part of my idea had worked. And Geri Stack was something to look at. The photograph had shown only her face, but the rest of her was special too.

We had a couple of drinks and talked about Dixieland jazz. I hadn't thought much about it in a long time, except that when I was tired, I'd go home and listen to Bix and the early Armstrong and Goodman, but it all came back as we talked. Then we ordered lunch, and she started talking about it and didn't even pretend. We were halfway through lunch when she pulled a fast one on me.

"Milo," she said, "you really know your Dixie—you never got it on a quick study—but I'd like to know why you wanted to pick me up so badly you broke that Armstrong platter."

She'd put it too straight. There was no point in trying to dodge. I took a long time answering. I wanted it to be right and I didn't want her to feel used.

"How did you guess? I asked her.

"I've been around," she said. "The door didn't hit you hard

enough for the spin you did. But I saw you straighten out long enough to put one heel on the record. You weren't really wide-eyed enough for a fan who wanted to have lunch with Geri Stack. Also, there's been a little light deep in your eyes all the time we talked."

"Maybe that was for you," I said.

She laughed. "I saw that light, too," she said. "The one I'm talking about was different. It was like a good blues note."

I finished the last of my lunch, stirred the sugar in my coffee, lit a cigarette, and looked at her. She was still waiting.

"It was a pick-up," I admitted. "But it's all on the level. I'll tell you the whole story, but I'd rather do it later. How about having dinner with me? Then I'll go to hear you sing, and afterwards we'll talk about it. Until then, I'd like it if we're just a man and a woman who were introduced by Louis Armstrong."

Now it was her turn to take a long time to answer.

"Louis always was unconventional," she said finally, and I knew it would be all right.

I took her back to her hotel in time for an interview and left her there. There was nothing more to be done until that night, so I went to a matinee movie and then spent the rest of the afternoon at a quiet bar.

That evening we had dinner together. By the time we arrived at the Groove Grove we were already old friends. It had been a long time since I had enjoyed myself so much. I'd almost forgotten that I was working.

The Groove Grove was a larger club, and it was already packed when we arrived. It was the most mixed crowd I'd ever seen. Negroes and whites. Café society and the beer nursers. Formal wear and bobby soxers. Gin-and-bitters and muggles. But they all had one thing in common. They loved jazz.

I had a table near the mike, where Geri could join me between numbers. After a while I got around to asking the waiter about Reet Coles. The waiter knew him and pointed to a table not far from me. He was a thin, pasty-faced man, expensively dressed in the tasteless fashion of so many hoods. I thought he was another needle man until I saw the cigarette he was smoking. Just to make sure, I got up and walked past him on the way to the men's room. A sharp, acrid odor bit into my nostrils as I passed him. It was marijuana. He was one of those who had to smoke up so he could concentrate on every pear-shaped note.

There was no question about Geri Stack. She was sending everyone in the place—even me. When she gave out with the "Jelly Roll Blues," I found myself getting the same dazed expression everyone else was wearing.

Afterwards, we slipped out the back way to avoid running the gauntlet. We stopped off for something to eat, and then I took her to the hotel.

She had a suite, with a refrigerator. And a bottle of brandy. I had brandy on the rocks, and she made herself a highball. We walked back into the living room and put the drinks down. I turned to look at her. I didn't remember either one of us moving, but suddenly she was in my arms. With an almost inaudible sigh, her mouth found mine.

Later, much later, I lit a cigarette and picked up my glass.

My brandy on the rocks had become brandy water. I went into the kitchenette and made two fresh drinks. I handed her one and sat down next to her on the studio couch.

"Slip me five," she said softly.

I reached down and held her hand.

"We're solid," she said.

"The best," I agreed. "Two cats standing over a broken record."

She laughed. It was still a nice laugh. She sipped her highball while I drank my brandy.

"Now," I said. I told her the idea I'd been working on. I knew it would be for her to make the connection with what had just happened, but I told her all of it. She didn't make anything out of it, except what was there. I even told her some of the remarks she might have to hear once or twice. But when I finished, she only nodded.

Five a.m. was coming up when I left Geri. One of my coat pockets had a bulge. She kissed me again at the door.

"See you tomorrow?" she asked. It was just a question, not a demand.

I shook my head. "Not until next day. Tomorrow will be it, or I'll be right back where I started."

"Be careful," she said, and closed the door.

I went home and went to sleep. Even my dreams were an improvement over what they'd been recently.

Something kept buzzing around my head like an angry bee. After a while I realized it was the phone. I tried to ignore it, but it wouldn't stop. Finally I opened my eyes and looked at the time. Eleven o'clock. I lit a cigarette and pulled on it another minute while the phone went on ringing. Finally I reached for it and picked up the receiver.

"Yeah?" I said.

"Milo, where the hell are you?" boomed a voice. It was Niels. If he'd opened his office window, I probably could have heard him just as well without the phone.

"Where am I?" I asked. "Where did you call?"

"Comedian," he snapped. "You drunk?"

"No, why?"

"So you had this thing all figured out?" he said. "So sure of yourself you just sleep through the day. It's got to be Willie Vander, and Willie Vander's dead, so there's nothing to worry about. That it?"

"What're you getting so hot about?" I asked.

"There's been another one. A singer named Geri Stack. She was robbed here last night. The same kind of phony story. Great Northern had her covered and they're screaming their heads off."

"Why?" I asked. "I said forty-eight hours, and that gives me another twenty to go."

"You're so smart," he said sarcastically, "maybe you know right away who pulled this one."

"I do," I said.

That stopped him for a second, but no more. "Who?" he demanded.

"I did."

This time there was a long silence. When he spoke, he'd eased up on the voice and was using the confidential tone he brings out when he thinks he's talking to someone a little off his rocker. "Milo," he said, "I know it's been a tough grind and I don't blame you for taking a drink or two—"

"I'm not drunk," I said. It was my turn to yell. "I took the girl's family jewels and I've got them right here with me. It's part of an idea and maybe it'll pay off if you keep your big mouth shut and your big feet out of the case."

"That's an idea?" he asked. "Milo, my boy, you got any idea how the insurance company is going to feel if they find out their own investigator has started lifting ice?"

"They'll probably lose their faith in human nature," I said dryly. "Just keep a grip on your upper plates and stop worrying. Nobody will ever know that I took them, except you and me and the girl."

"She knows?" he asked. "How do you know she won't break? How do you—"

"Niels," I said firmly, "there's a guy at the door selling Cadillacs, and I want to buy a couple before he gets away. Just hold on." I put the receiver down on the table and went back to sleep.

It was the middle of the afternoon when I awakened again. I put the receiver back on the hook and made myself some breakfast. After breakfast, I had some more coffee and then went in and finished a book I'd started reading a week before. The phone rang, but I ignored it. I played some solitaire. Then I broke out a bottle of brandy and started a new book. Around seven o'clock I scrounged in the refrigerator and found enough to fix myself a dinner of sorts.

Just before nine, I decided it was time to move. I took a

shower, shaved, and got dressed. I went over the .38 to see that it was working, and strapped on the shoulder holster. Then I dug under some clean shirts in my dresser and got out the reserve forces. This was an old-fashioned, four-barreled derringer I'd picked up a long time ago. A gunsmith had fixed it so it would fire .32-caliber shells. I'd had a little harness made for it so it would clip under the edge of my coat. It worked something like a magician's gimmick; all I had to do was press my arm against the clip, and the tiny gun would drop into my hand.

I wrapped the jewels up in a neat package and I was ready. I went downstairs and got into my car and headed downtown. I stopped off once to send a telegram. Then I drove straight to the Groove Grove.

It was too early for the big crowd and too early for Geri Stack. But a number of the characters were already there, and I spotted Reet Coles standing at the bar and sipping on a beer. I crowded in next to him and ordered a double brandy. I knew he was looking at me, and my guess was that he'd remember that I'd been with Geri Stack the night before. But I paid no attention.

When my drink came, I picked it up and then looked around. Coles was still looking at me, and I could see the wheels turning. I decided I might as well give them an extra push right then. I raised the brandy higher.

"To Willie Vander?" I repeated. We were both keeping our voices down so no one else could hear us. "I'll tell you, chum. Because he's dead. You know about it,"

"I read the newspapers," he said carefully. He was trying to figure it fast enough to get a step ahead of me.

"Sure, you read," I said. I let it get nasty. "You're a big boy,"

There was a glitter in his eyes, but they went blank again. "You looking for something?" he asked.

"Nothing from you, baby," I said. "But you can do yourself a favor."

He waited.

"When I case a town," I said, "I case the competition. I know all about Willie Vander."

"Why tell me?" he asked, "Maybe the cops would like to see you,"

"Sure they would," I said with a laugh. "But you're Reet Coles."

"Reet," he said. It was the way he'd gotten his name. By saying it that way.

"Like I said, I know all about Willie Vander. I know who his friends were and who he saw. That's how I know you're Reet Coles. The last job, Willie Vander got the jump on me. I was lined up on it, too, but he got there first. The dancer, the one with the sparkling belly button."

"The Jelly Roll heist," he said. It was sort of an admission, but not much of one.

"Yeah," I said. "I knew Willie Vander's last job and I knew his next one. If he'd lived, he would've lost the jump on that one."

"You talk a lot," he said. "You got a name?"

"That's not what I'm selling," I said, "You want to look or you want to go on showing me how bright you can talk?"

He shrugged his shoulders. "If there's a character in town, he comes to the Grove. I don't know what you're chewing up your lip about, chum, but I might as well take a look. Then maybe you'll shut up."

"Where?" I asked.

He turned and walked toward the men's room. I followed him. When we got there, it was empty. He leaned with his back against the door and looked at me. I tore a hole in one end of the package and let him look. There was enough showing to give him the idea.

"Seems there was something in the papers today about Geri Stack losing her jewels," he said slowly. "You were in here with her last night and you left with her. Maybe the cops would like to know that."

"Maybe," I said. I made like I was going to put the package in my pocket. His eyes followed the package, and then it was too late. I had the .38 out, and the nose of it was against his belt buckle.

He let his breath out with a harsh sound. "Put it away," he said. "I'm no pigeon. My wings are too short."

I looked him over and then put the gun away. We stood like that for another minute.

"So you're a guy walking around with his family jewels," he said. "Why tell me about it?"

"I want to put them in circulation," I said. "Besides, I'm ambitious, and Willie Vander is dead. I like to work with a big outfit, and I figure maybe they need a new boy. Unless they're yellowing and going to quit with chicken feed."

"You ought to take up tea," he said. "You'd really be fighting them off. Come on, my beer's going stale back there."

We went out of the men's room and back toward the bar. I

knew I'd started something, but I still didn't know if it was what I wanted.

"Buy yourself another drink," he said when we reached the bar. I ordered another brandy and let my breath out. He was going to call someone, and I was willing to bet they'd at least want to look me over. After about five minutes he came back to stand beside me.

"You want to go for a ride?" he asked me.

"Why not?" I said. I finished my brandy. "But don't get any bright ideas. You're not big enough to take me."

He gave me a crooked grin and led the way outside. He had a big car, and when he started the motor, I could tell that the engine had been souped up. It was like throwing fire on fire. But he kept it under wraps as we drove out of the parking lot.

He was heading the right way. As soon as I saw that, I leaned back and relaxed, trying to breathe as little as possible. Inside the car, the smell of marijuana was enough to make me cough.

It was a thirty-minute drive to the sanatorium. We made it in twenty. A collection of fairly modern buildings clustered inside a high brick wall. The place had been there for several years. Lew Mora, in spite of being one of the crown princes of Eastern gangdom, was a doctor. I'd heard that he'd never even lost his license to practice in New York. Part of the sanatorium was on the level, too. They had around two hundred lungers there, and the rumor was that they were well treated.

The sanatorium belonged to Joe Rinchetti, a big wheel in the crime syndicate. He'd rated considerable mention in the Kefauver hearings. A lot of people believed that a part of the sanatorium was used for something other than lungers—that guys who were hot could hole up there, for a price. The state police had gone looking for customers a couple of times, but had drawn blanks.

Reet Coles drove past the main entrance and pulled up in front of a smaller gate. A guy peered out, and Reet waved to him. The gate swung open, the electric lock controlled from inside. I sat there, hoping I was as smart as it seemed I was that afternoon.

The car stopped in front of one of the smaller buildings, and we got out. Reet Coles rang the bell. There was a long wait. I didn't try to spot it, but I knew there was a peephole somewhere and that I was probably being looked over.

The door swung open. The man who stood there was about fifty. He wore a smoking jacket and heavy black-rimmed glasses. He carried a book in his hand, one finger marking his place. Just a nice, respectable character, greeting late visitors.

"Ah, Mr. Coles," he said. He peered at me. "And a friend. Come in."

We stepped inside and followed him into a comfortable study. He went around behind the desk and sat down.

"Does your friend have a name, Mr. Coles?" he asked.

"If he does, he's keeping it under wraps," Reet Coles said. "But this is the guy, Doc. He claims he heisted the Stack dame last night. He was with her, all right, and he's got some stuff that looks like what she was wearing. And he's loaded."

"Oh?" Dr. Mora said. He looked at me with interest. "I don't suppose you'd care to tell me who you are?"

"I've already told what I've got," I said. "Maybe I'll give more information after I get a little."

"Understandable," he murmured. "But first, just so we may operate with some mutual trust, will you please give me your gun? It will be returned when you leave."

I didn't like that, but I wasn't ready for a showdown. I took the .38 out slowly and carefully, and put it on his desk. He slid it into an open drawer.

"Now," he said, "perhaps you'd like to show me the merchandise you claim you have."

Casually I tossed the package on the desk. He opened it and spread the jewels out. He took out a jeweler's loupe and examined them. Twice he stopped and looked at a list on his desk. They were careful boys. They knew in advance what they were going to get. Finally he looked up and nodded.

"What do you want?" he asked.

"I want to put them in circulation." I said. "After that, maybe we can work up a future for ourselves."

He gave me a humorless smile. "Let me ask you a question," he said. "Suppose I decide I want to keep these and not pay for them? Suppose I decide you have no future?"

"That's two questions," I said. "You could do it, but I don't think you're that stupid."

"Why?"

"Look at what you've got," I said. "About a million bucks in jewelry. You might squeeze a couple hundred grand out of the insurance companies for a return with no questions. Or, if you fence them, you might get fifty grand. That's cigarette money. And Willie Vander is dead."

"You think you could step into Willie's shoes?"

"Why not?" I asked carelessly. "I proved it last night. And I'm smarter than Willie. If I had the setup he had, I wouldn't show off just to prove I could pick up rocks as easy as the guy whose job it was. This is small stuff around here. If it works that well, why not move in on New York? Then there's London, Paris, Cannes."

"You know what happened to Willie Vander?" he asked. But I could tell he was interested.

"I know," I said. "I even know why. Like I said, it was partly the belly dancer. Willie broke the routine there. He had to show he was smart. It put the finger on him. The cops got close, or maybe the insurance dick, and it was safer to pay Willie off."

"You're smart," Lew Mora said. "How come I haven't seen you around before if you're so smart?"

"I've been away," I said. "Now you're seeing me."

"Suppose I said okay? Suppose I said we'll take you on?"

"That's not saying anything. I knew Willie Vander. I cased him. I knew he saw the tea kid here. I had an idea he came out this way once in a while. But I don't know that. Maybe he went somewhere else. Maybe you want to step into somebody else's shoes like I want to step into Willie's."

"I'm Lew Mora," he said. He said it the way a guy would announce he was Winston Churchill.

"I've heard of you," I said, underplaying it. "I know you've got a finger in a lot of things. Notch houses. Happy stuff. Sucker rolls. One-armed bandits. But I don't know that Lew Mora had anything to do with Willie Vander."

"What do you want?" he asked.

I pretended to think it over. Then I pretended to have an idea. "I cased a lot of the jobs Willie was on," I said. "I knew all about them, but he got there first. I'd know some of the stuff. You show it to me and then we'll talk business."

He got up from the desk and walked to a door on the other side of the study. He opened it. "Joe," he said, "come in a minute."

It was Joe Rinchetti. I'd seen his pictures enough times to know him. He was big and fat. Little black eyes peered out of the folds of fat with about the same animation as two raisins in a lump of dough. Expensive clothes and a diamond ring like a searchlight didn't conceal that he'd come up, and stayed, the hard way.

"Yeah, Lew?" he said. He was looking at me.

"We got a guy here," Lew Mora said. "He's smart and he talks tough. He'd like to try on Willie Vander's shoes for size."

Rinchetti was still looking at me. "Know you from somewhere?" he asked.

We'd never met, and I was hoping he'd never seen me anywhere. "I don't think so," I said. "Dannemora? Joliet?"*

"Not me," he said with pride. "But I never forget a face." He continued to stare at me but spoke to Lew Mora. "You like him for it, Lew?"

"He has qualifications," Lew Mora said. "But he wants to be sure he doesn't tie in with a bunch of amateurs. He's shown us what he's got. Now he wants to see what we have."

Rinchetti made a gesture of contempt. "Show him," he said.

_____

* Dannemora is the Clinton Correctional Facility in New York State. Joliet Correctional Center in Illinois closed in 2002.

But he continued to stare at me. I was beginning to feel like a turkey the day before Thanksgiving.

Lew Mora walked across the room and slid aside a section of books. There was a safe there. He twirled the dial while I kept my gaze away from the safe and tried to pretend that I didn't know that Joe Rinchetti was still watching me.

When the safe door swung open, Lew Mora reached inside and came out with both hands full and dumped them on his desk. It was like seeing a close-up of the Milky Way. I'd gone over the descriptions enough to recognize some of the pieces.

"Okay," I said. "Let's talk about Willie's shoes. Have you set up contact for dealing with the insurance companies, or do we have to fence them?

"Insurance," Joe Rinchetti said suddenly. His voice was harsher. "I remember now. Lew, you remember when we set this up, we brought Randy in from New York? He cased all the local insurance people and then made like a sidewalk photographer until he got pictures of all of them. That's where I seen this guy. He's an insurance dick."

I backed up against the bookcase fast. There are times when you can go on bluffing and there are times when you can't. With these guys it was already later than any clock could show. There wasn't going to be any long conversation before they pulled the trigger. Still, I made one more try.

"Yeah," I said. "The name is Milo March." I could tell they recognized that. "But don't jump to conclusions. Maybe I can still fill Willie Vander's shoes."

"You can," Lew Mora said. "The shoes he was wearing yesterday morning,"

I waited, trying to watch all three of them at the same time. I'd gambled on time, and it looked as if it had just hopped into the double zero.

"You want to take him, Reet?" Rinchetti said.

"Reet," said the pasty-faced guy. He reached for this gun with obvious enjoyment. You could see that he needed a smoke, and maybe this was going to give him the same lift for a minute or two.

Neither Lew Mora nor Joe Rinchetti had gotten where they were by being slow. Lew already had a desk drawer open and was clawing out a gun at the same time he was dropping behind the desk. I steadied the derringer and shot. I saw the hole in his forehead before he flopped out of sight.

Something struck my left shoulder and spun me around. I felt something, not much worse than the first shot of Novocain—then. The sound of the shot seemed to come much later. I straightened up and focused my eyes on Rinchetti. He was ready for another shot. I could see his finger whitening against the trigger. I pulled mine first.

He looked surprised. He tried to shoot again, but he was reaching for his belly with the hand that held the gun. His second bullet plowed into the rug, and he fell on top of it.

I turned back to look a Reet Coles. He was still standing up. He'd dropped his gun and was just standing there, shaking. It must have been a whole minute before I realized I'd missed him completely.

The doorbell rang.

"Anyone else in here?" I asked him.

He shook his head. I stepped to the desk, slipping the derringer in my pocket, and picked my .38 out of the drawer. I crumpled the paper package around the things I'd brought and stuck them in my pocket. The bell rang again.

"Go ahead and open the door," I told him. I followed behind him. My shoulder was beginning to hurt, and I could feel the blood spreading.

Coles opened the door. There was practically an army outside—Selsden of Robbery, Malikoff of Homicide, and a bunch of guys in state uniforms.

"It took you long enough," I said.

Murray Malikoff said acidly, "Maybe, after this, you won't wait until the last minute to tell me what you're doing. I had to get Selsden, we had to get the state boys, and then we had to wake up a judge and get a paper. What's happened?"

"Go look," I said, pointing toward the study. I didn't feel like making long explanations. One of them took Reet Coles off my hand, and the others crowded into the study. I followed slowly.

"It's all there," I said to Selsden when I could get his attention. I indicated the desk.

"I see it," he said. He indicated the side of my coat. I looked down and saw a bracelet half out of my pocket. "What's that, Milo?"

"Bait," I said. "I brought them and I'll take them. They belong to a girl who stuck her neck out to help. I want that made clear. She was a big help to you."

"Stack?" he asked.

I nodded. It seemed to me the lights in the place were

getting dimmer. Then I realized what it was. I tried to make it to a chair, but I couldn't quite do it.

"He's been shot," I heard someone say, and I hit the floor. Now, that was a great observation.

It turned out that the bullet had gone cleanly through my shoulder. No bones were touched. The police doctor fixed it up and suggested that I go to the hospital. Instead I went to a hotel.

The next day the papers did a big spread on how Geri Stack had pretended to be robbed in order to help Lieutenant Selsden. There was no mention of Milo March, which was just the way I wanted it.

Niels Bancroft was so happy he gave me a three-week vacation to get over being shot. The first two weeks were fine. Then Geri Stack had to move on to another engagement, and that was no fun. I moped around my apartment, drank brandy, and got bored.

There was one thing about the last robbery that had kept bothering me. When I got bored, I got to thinking about it again. Finally I decided I had to find out. I went over to Little Egypt one night and got a table in the back. I watched the floor show. When it was over, I skirted the tables and went back. I knocked on the door.

"*Giriniz,*" a voice called through the door. I went into the dressing room. She was lying on a couch, resting. She had on her costume, and this time the ten-carat ruby was back in its place. She still looked as beautiful as she had the first time.

"Hello," she said, and she remembered not to use the accent. "I wondered if you'd ever come around again." She made room for me to sit beside her on the couch.

"I got scratched a little, getting it back," I said. I touched the ruby with the tip of my finger. I could tell that it was pretty solid.

Her eyes had gotten brighter. "I haven't thanked you yet," she said.

"In Turkey," I said, "they say *'Te ekkür ederim'*—or do like this."

I leaned over and kissed her. Her mouth was like cold fire, but there was nothing cold about the way it crushed against mine.

The warning buzzer for the next floor show had already sounded when I lit two cigarettes and handed one to her.

"I'll be back later," I said, "but I came early because I was curious about something."

"Yes?" she asked.

"Yes," I said. I tossed the ruby back to her. "We'll forget the shop talk when I come back."

She was laughing as I left the dressing room.

2

Hair the Color of Blood

I came in on the Denver flight to the Los Angeles International Airport. A taxi took me to the Monica-Wilshire, in Santa Monica. On Ocean Avenue, facing the Pacific through the lace of kingly palm trees, it is a swank hotel; and in California, when something is swank, they put it on with a trowel. In addition to the regular rooms, there was a double row of bungalow rooms out under the palm trees. I took one of the bungalows, at fifteen dollars a day. Too rich for my blood, but I was going to pretend I could afford it.

It was the beginning of my two-week vacation. I was in a to-hell-with-business-bring-on-the-girls mood, and I was going to enjoy myself if it killed me. It almost did.

I tipped the bellboy enough to give a small-type midget old-age security. He did everything but kiss my hand, and left. I bounced on the bed just to get the feel of luxury.

That was when the woman screamed. It was a high, shrill scream, as if somebody had made an improper advance to a steam whistle. It was filled with terror. Then it shut off too quickly. It had come from the bungalow directly behind mine. Before I could remind myself that I was on vacation, I was outside and heading for the end of the row of bungalows.

The door of the corner bungalow opened and a girl looked out. She had red hair that curled down to her shoulders. She was wearing a bikini bathing suit that left little to the imagination—but imagination could never have matched the real thing. It almost made me forget the scream.

"Did you hear someone scream?" she asked me.

I stopped taking inventory and looked at her face. "I think it was on the other side," I said. "I was just going to take a look." I hoped my voice indicated I could be talked out of it. She did the next-best thing. "Stop and tell me about it on the way back," she said.

"Sure," I agreed, taking another look to be sure the bikini hadn't moved; then I went around the corner.

The bungalows were built in a double row, back to back. I stopped in front of the third door, which would be the one right behind mine. My better sense told me to go back to the redhead and forget about the scream—but if I'd *had* any better sense, I would have stayed in my bungalow. I knocked.

The door was opened by a man. He was young, maybe in his thirties, and good-looking, if you like the George Raft type. He had his coat off, but he was wearing one of those fancy vests you see around these days. This one was really blinding. It was canary yellow with red stitching.

"Sorry to bother you," I said, "but I heard somebody screaming. Anything I can do to help?"

Now that I was there, I felt a little foolish about the whole thing. I expected him to tell me I could mind my own business, then slam the door in my face. Instead he gave me a grin that had been wound a little too tight.

ILLUSTRATION BY AL TARTER

"It was my wife," he said. "She cut herself. I'm sorry she disturbed you, Mr. ..."

"March." I said. "Milo March."

"The least we can do," he said, "is offer you a drink in return for your offering to help. Won't you come in?"

Sometimes you'll do something that even as you're doing it you know is a mistake. That's the way it was with me. I stepped into the bungalow, knowing damn well there was something wrong with the setup. There was.

Out of the corner of my eye I saw him move, and I tried to duck. But I was a little too late. Something cracked against my head, there was an echo of pain inside, and that was all. I didn't even feel myself hit the floor.

The next thing I knew, my head was hurting. That was all I knew for at least a minute. I was lying down and my head hurt. I struggled with that for another minute before I remembered why my head hurt. I hadn't opened my eyes yet. I could feel something across the lower part of my legs and I could feel a sheet under me. So I was probably in bed without any clothes on, because I realized the sheet was rubbing against bare skin. My first thought was that somebody had found me and taken me to my room. I opened my eyes to check on it.

The first thing I saw was a magenta cover twisted around my feet. The cover on my bed had been pink. I remembered that much. It wasn't my room, so it must be the one belonging to the guy with the fancy vest. I raised up on one elbow to look for him. What I saw made me forget all about my headache.

I was in bed with a woman. Both of us were stripped right down to the buff. Her buff must have been pretty nice in its day, but she was already a few years past her day. She had long red hair. Not like the girl in the bikini; this one's hair was dark red, like blood. Her throat was the same color. Somebody had slashed it until you could have shoved a fist into it—if you weren't particular where you shoved your fist.

No wonder she'd stopped screaming. Her neck was cut half-way through. There was blood all over the place, including a few generous smears on my chest. I lifted my hand and it was covered with blood I just made it to the bathroom. Then I was sick. It's not that I can't stand the sight of blood, but the knock on the head plus the feel of the drying blood on my hand had been too much. Suddenly my stomach was as sensitive as a careless bride's.

I felt weak, but a little better when I finished. My head had settled down to a steady throb. I was about to wash up when a key rattled in the door and it swung open. Two cops and a bellhop came in.

"Jeez," the bellhop said when he saw me. "He's a fast worker. He checked in only a half hour ago and here he—" He looked at the bed and his face turned green.

The two cops were ahead of him. They'd already seen what was on the bed, and they were coming for me. Both of them looked a little tight around the face.

"Take it easy," I told them. "I can explain everything."

"This is going to take some explaining," one of them said dryly.

When I thought about it, I had to admit he was right. I told them my story. It went over like a strip act at a convention of bishops. I sounded silly even to me, but then I was at a disadvantage. It's pretty hard to do any formal talking when everyone else is dressed and you're stark naked.

I threw in the business about the redhead in the end bungalow. That would at least place me outside of the room before the woman screamed.

"You mean One-B?" the bellhop asked. "There's nobody in there. It's been empty for two days."

"Like hell it's empty," I said. "I never saw a room so well filled."

"Check on it, Joe," one of the cops said to the other.

He was back in two minutes, shaking his head. "It's empty," he said. After that we sat around in an unfriendly silence, waiting for the detectives to arrive. I wanted to get dressed, but they wouldn't hear of it. They liked me the way I was as well as they would ever like me.

The deluge came in a few minutes. Homicide cops, identification men, and a couple of men from the coroner's office.

The two patrolmen and the bellhop got lost in the shuffle. They kept me shoved in a corner while they went over the room. They found the knife on the floor—on the side of the bed I'd been on. They dusted the whole place for prints. One of the men came over and printed me. Then they photographed everything, including me—cheesecake, yet!

When they'd finished that, the coroner's men started to take her out in a basket. One of the detectives got big-hearted: he let me get washed and put my clothes on. Then we started all over again. But this time they started out by asking for my identification.

I told them and showed them. Milo March, thirty-five years old, Chief Investigator for the Trans-World Insurance Service Corporation in Denver. Six feet tall. One hundred and eighty-five pounds. A gun permit for Denver, Colorado. Another gun permit for Los Angeles. I'd been out there the year before on a job, but the gun permit was still good.

Finally they got around to my story.

I told it a little better this time, fortified by clothes, but it was a cold audience.

After that we went down to Headquarters and I told my tired little story again. They went to work on it piecemeal. They took turns going over the ground with me. Back and forth, like a couple dancing to a broken record.

There are two kinds of cops when it comes to questioning. There are the ones who back up their questions with a nightstick wrapped in a towel. Then there are the cops who are polite but keep you under a strong light and just keep you talking. The first kind is worse for the first few hours; after that they're both about the same. These were polite cops. Nobody raised his voice or pointed a finger at me. But they kept me telling the same story over and over again until I was so sick of it I was thinking of changing it just to brighten up the day. The way things looked, it could stand a little brightening.

They didn't learn any more than I'd told them the first time, but I learned a couple of things. The dead woman was named Sherry Azana, and she'd registered alone at the hotel. Once she'd been a showgirl. More recently she'd been the girlfriend of six or seven big-spending mobsters. For the past two months she'd been in hiding.

Somewhere along the course, an FBI man dropped in to listen to me. They were interested in the girl, too. It seemed the local cops and the government had an idea she might talk a few men into jail, if they could only get her. Apparently some of the men had had the same idea—and they'd reached her first.

I told them about the guy who'd opened the door, but it didn't make much of a dent. I had to admit that the description could fit a lot of people.

Finally the atmosphere changed a little. Things weren't breaking for me, but they were bending. They talked to a couple of cops in Denver by phone and heard I was a good boy. They heard the same thing from a Los Angeles cop who knew me. They verified the time I'd arrived at the airport. Better yet, the coroner reported that Sherry Azana's throat had been cut from right to left, meaning the knife had been held in the killer's left hand. They proved to themselves that

I was right-handed. Some other bright boy in their lab studied the pictures and said the blood on me had been smeared there instead of spurting onto me.

It wasn't much, but the way things looked, I needed all I could get.

"We could hold you, March," one of the detectives finally said. "You're a hell of a long way from being in the clear, but I'll admit there's a reasonable doubt. Several guys have said you're okay, so we're going to let you go. But stick around where we can find you when we want you."

"Sure," I said. I was so tired I didn't much care whether they let me go or not. "I'm on vacation, remember? They tell me there's nothing like the tan you can get from the reflections off a cop's badge. Only don't overdo it. I don't want to get burned."

"We don't burn them here; we gas them," he said reassuringly.*

On that cheerful note, I left. It was just ten hours since they had taken me down there; it felt like ten days.

I went straight back to the hotel and went to bed. But my fifteen-dollar room was wasted that day. The way I felt, I could have slept just as soundly in the gutter.

I slept twelve hours without even turning over. Then I had some breakfast and a double shot of brandy brought in. By the time I'd put that away, I felt better. I finally got around to my problem.

One day of my vacation was gone. I didn't want to spend the rest of it playing footsie with the cops. I'd been working

---

* In present-day California, lethal gas is a secondary execution method only (after lethal injection).

the same side of the street long enough to know that some-times the cops don't get the right guy. Besides, I didn't like being a patsy for any guy in a fancy yellow vest. I wanted to know two things: where the guy was, and how the other redhead fit into the picture—the girl in the bikini who'd been in the room that wasn't occupied.

There was a car-rental place across the street from the hotel. I could have my choice of one Ford or seven Cadillacs. Being a modest man, I took a Cadillac so no one would know I was a tourist. Anyway, it figured. Anywhere else you'd say that the condemned man ate a hearty meal; in California you'd say he took a ride in a Cadillac.

I drove down to Beverly Hills and found the most expen-sive men's shop. I went in and asked about fancy yellow vests, describing the one I'd seen.

"Just a minute," the salesman said. He went into the rear and came back with a yellow vest. It was a duplicate of the one I'd seen on the guy who sapped me. "You mean this one?"

"That's it," I said. "Don't tell me every store in town has it."

"Hardly," he said with a smile that was meant to say that not everyone would appreciate this item. He was right. "In fact, sir, I doubt if more than ten shops will carry this partic-ular line. And it is not for sale yet."

That sounded more interesting. "What does that mean?" I asked.

"These are advance samples of a line we're getting from England in a few months. We have one of each model so we can take advance orders. The same applies to the other stores, I'm sure."

He gave me the name of the man through whom they'd ordered the vests. I thanked him and left.

I found the wholesaler in. He was a little cagey at first, but I flashed my identification and gave him a fast line about insurance investigations, and he finally came across with the list. There were twelve stores that had samples of the yellow vest. That made it a little easier than I had expected it to be.

Starting in Los Angeles, I began to work my way west. The first four stores were certainly blanks. They showed me their sample yellow number, and in each case it obviously hadn't been worn. And there was no one around who looked like my boy.

The fifth shop was on Sunset Boulevard, between Los Angeles and Beverly Hills—the Strip. It was a place called "Hollywood's Fancy." All I had was the name and the address. But I could guess what it looked like. Everything on the Strip had a certain air. The nightclubs looked like small palaces; the stores always reminded me of someone dressed up but with no place to go; while the offices of agents, outnumbering everything else, had the look and smell of high-priced brothels.

When I found the store, it looked exactly as I expected it would. The display windows were filled with fifty-dollar ties and hundred-dollar suede jackets. I went in, expecting to find another velvet-voiced clerk who would look at my two-dollar tie as if it had polio.* But it wasn't like that at all. As soon as I saw the two clerks, I knew that I had finally come to the right place.

---

* Polio was prominent in public awareness at the time of this story's publication in July 1953; 1952 had been the worst year of the epidemic. Salk's vaccine was announced in March 1953, and trials began in 1954.

They both looked like undergraduates at San Quentin. One of them was blond and one was dark-haired, one was short and the other tall—but they still looked as if they were cut from the same pattern. It was in the way they moved, in the lack of expression on their faces. When they looked at me, all they saw was the outline of a target. You can find their kind wherever there's an opportunity for a slow brain to make a fast buck. The fact that they were wearing $200 suits did not do a thing for them except accent it. The coats had been cut by a good tailor, but he hadn't been good enough to conceal the guns in the shoulder holsters.

They were sitting back of the counter, playing cards. They looked up and through me as I entered.

"Just window-shopping." I smiled.

"Then do it outside," one of them said flatly. "We don't sell no windows." Their expressions didn't change, but it was obvious they thought this was very funny.

"How about fancy vests?" I asked.

"Beat it," one of them said. "We're busy. Besides, we got all the dummies we need."

I walked over and looked at a rack of ties. "I'm looking for a guy. He's left-handed. Yesterday he was wearing a yellow vest that was imported from England. He used to have a girl-friend named Sherry."

You could feel the atmosphere change in the place. They'd lost their interest in cards. I was getting as much attention as Marilyn Monroe at a Junior Prom.

"Yeah?" one of them rasped. "What about it?"

"Him and his girlfriend," I said. "She was thinking of taking up singing. He figured it might hurt his social position, so the next time he met her, he cut her dead."

They tightened up a little more. "Who are you?"

"I," I said in my best YMCA voice, "am the founder of the Society for the Preservation of the Memory of Sherry Azana. I'm recruiting charter members."

They looked at each other; then their eyes swung back to me. "A wise guy!" one of them said. "Go tell Fancy."

The second one went back and slipped through a door in the rear of the store. The other one stayed to watch me.

The other man came back. "The boss wants to see him," he said.

"You loaded, pal?" my watchdog asked. He got up and came around the counter. His eyes were bright enough to use in a Murine ad.

I shook my head. I wasn't being exactly truthful. I'd left my .38 in my suitcase, but I'd stuck a small gun in my pocket. It was an old four-barreled derringer. I'd had it rebored so it would take a .32. It was always nice to have four extra shots. And it was small enough to fit in the palm of my hand. I stuck both of my hands in my pockets, curling one hand around the gun. I wasn't ready for a showdown yet, but I didn't want to lose it either.

He gave me a fast patting. He even patted the pocket where my hand was, but he was looking for a regular gun that couldn't have been covered by a hand.

"You've got a nice touch," I told him. "Maybe we could go steady."

He wasn't amused. "Inside," he said, motioning me toward the door.

As I went through, I could see this was a soundproofed room. Then I turned my attention to other matters.

"He's clean, Fancy," one of the men said.

The office was in the Hollywood tradition. It was furnished with the best. The rug was so thick and soft you couldn't have made time across it without snowshoes. There were a couple of big leather chairs. The desk was covered with leather, too. And back of it was the guy I was looking for. He was wearing a fawn-colored suede vest instead of the yellow number, but it was the same boy.

Now I knew why he'd looked a little familiar when I saw him the day before. The name "Fancy" had jogged my memory. I'd seen his picture. This was Frank Bradford, better known as Fancy Bradford. The crime syndicate had sent him in to replace Mickey Cohen when the Feds awarded Mickey an all-expense vacation.* Fancy Bradford was the number one man on the West Coast. I was traveling in fast company.

There was one thing I hadn't noticed the day before: there were a couple of scratches high on one cheek. They looked like ones that might have been made by nails.

I'd wondered if he would pretend he'd never seen me before, but he didn't bother. He was grinning up at me. The day before, his smile had been tight, but then it was a squeeze play. Today he was top dog again and his grin showed it. The morning papers were on his desk.

"Is this the guy, Fancy?" one of the men asked.

"This is the guy," Fancy said. "Milo March, insurance dick,

---

* As a result of the Kefauver investigations, Cohen was sent to prison in 1952 for tax evasion. Bradford is a fictional character.

self-appointed Boy Scout and sucker. Milo, meet the boys—Lance Harker and Barry Alfama." Lance Harker was the tall one.

"I've already met the boys," I said. "They're sweet."

The "boys" scowled and Fancy laughed. "Sit down," he said, gesturing toward the leather chairs.

I was going to say no; then I had an idea. I sat down in one of the chairs. It was like sitting on a cloud. I took my hand out of my pocket and thrust it down between the cushion and the chair. The leather was as soft as a baby's thigh.

"How'd you get out?" he asked.

"Walked," I said. "It's not that I'm particular, but it seemed silly to stay in jail when I was paying for a good room. Besides, I wanted to find a guy who was wearing a yellow vest. I owed him something, and I like to pay my debts."

"Don't strain yourself," he said. "It'll be healthier. How much do you know?"

"Enough. You killed her because you thought she might talk. I'd guess she had so much on you that you didn't even want one of your men doing the job. ... What's the matter with your cheek? Cut yourself while shaving?"

His fingers passed over the scratches.

"The bitch!" he said. Then he stopped, remembering, and his gaze came back to me. "You tell the cops about me?"

"Only a rough description," I said. "I didn't know yesterday who you were. They didn't buy much of it—said it could be a thousand guys."

"And now?" His voice was gentle, but it wasn't soft. "How much do you want?"

"I got news for you, Fancy," I said. "There ain't many of us, but I'm one of those guys who doesn't want your money for any reason. Maybe you wear imported vests and two-hundred-buck suits, but in my book you're still a bum. A cheap bum."

He didn't like that. His eyes brightened. "You think you're going to the cops?" he asked. His voice was wearing a sneer. "It's a waste of time. I've got an alibi, a good one. I've beat tougher homicide raps than this one. Maybe the frame won't stay on you, but it can't be hung back on me. And if you nose around too much, maybe I'll let it be two raps to beat."

"Maybe I'll go to the cops," I said. I stood up. "Maybe I won't. Maybe I'll handle it myself. I don't like being pushed around by punks—even fancy punks."

For just a second he looked uncertain, his gaze darting at his two men.

"I told you he was clean," Lance Harker said. "I shook him down. Nothing, he's a tourist."

"Okay," Fancy said. His eyes came back to meet mine. They were like black granite. "You're lucky, March. You're lucky I don't have the boys dust you right here. Or do it myself. Now get out before I change my mind. And stay out."

"Sure," I said. I went to the door and opened it. Then I looked back at the three of them. "You've had your fun, Fancy. That was a real pretty frame, for an ad-lib—and it almost worked. But the next one's going to be on me. Don't make any dates too far ahead."

I went on out without waiting for an answer. I felt a little shaky in the knees. But I'd found my boy and I'd set the stage for the next step. Only it would have to be fast, while Fancy Bradford was still trying to make up his mind about me.

I got in my rented Caddy and drove off. When I was about a block away, another car pulled from the curb. I tried a change of pace and it matched me. I grinned to myself and ignored it after that.

There were a few nightclubs on the Strip that had smart money in them. I remembered them from the year before. I stopped in at each one and asked a few questions about Fancy. Everybody knew him, but nobody had anything to say. I'd expected that. All I wanted was to have somebody report back that I was asking.

I also asked some questions about another redhead, one with hair the color of red gold. I thought maybe she was Fancy's new girlfriend. But nobody knew anything about her either. I got the impression they were telling the truth about her, and that puzzled me.

I turned and went back up the Strip. When I hit Beverly Hills. I cut over to Wilshire, making sure I didn't lose the guy following me. Then I went straight out Wilshire to Santa Monica. I stopped at the police station. The other car parked a block behind me and stayed there as I went inside.

I asked for Lieutenant Blair Little. He was the guy who'd questioned me the night before. They kept me waiting for a few minutes, then told me where to find him. I went back to his office.

"Decided to come in and confess?" he asked.

"I never confess on Saturdays," I said. "I had a great-grand-father who was a Seventh-Day Adventist. You just made me feel so much at home that I had to come back."

He eyed me steadily. "Sure. What do you want, March?"

"Sherry Azana's things," I said. "You still got them around?"

"You think I take them home for my kids?" he asked sourly. "Why do you want to know?"

"Can I look at them?"

"Why?" he asked again.

"You know how it is," I said. "When you're in the business you can't stop thinking. Maybe I'll get an idea."

He grunted something under his breath, but he got up and led the way into the lab. In a minute, I was looking at all that was left of a girl everybody had thought would talk: Her clothes, all of them expensive. Her purse, with the usual assortment of powder and lipstick and perfume. Again, all expensive. A wallet with several hundred dollars in it. Some keys. Three rings, two of them with diamonds big enough to be searchlights, the other with an emerald. A watch with small diamonds set all around it. I turned the watch over. On the back of it there was some small engraving: *It took Sherry's fancy.* I was willing to bet a guy named Fancy Bradford had once thought that was real clever.

When the Lieutenant wasn't looking, I palmed the watch. Then I pushed the rest of the stuff back toward the lab man. "Nothing there," I said.

"What were you expecting to find?" he asked as we walked out.

"A clue," I answered. "You know, 'Quick, Watson, the needle'*—and all that sort of thing."

---

* A common misquote of Sherlock Holmes's words "Oh, Watson—the needle!" (referring to Holmes's drug habit), which conclude the 1939 film *The Hound of the Baskervilles*. This line is not in the novel.

He grunted something under his breath again.

"You been looking into any other suspects?" I asked him. "Or are you just sticking to me?"

"We had about ten of them in this morning," he said. "All of them with alibis and high-priced lawyers following on their heels. You know, one of them might fit the description you gave. I thought about it later. I think we'll invite him over again and have you take a look at him."

"Yeah?" I said without much interest.

"He had an alibi, too, but maybe it could be worked on if you recognize him. His name is Fancy Bradford."

"Fancy Bradford?" I said as if I'd never heard it before. "You know, Lieutenant, if anyone pinned a name like that on me, I wouldn't wait for the State to gas me—I'd do it myself. ... Tell me something else, Lieutenant."

"That's all I'm here for," he said wearily.

"Did the coroner find any skin scraping under her finger-nails?"

His eyes brightened with interest on that, but he wasn't giving anything away. "Did you find some scratches on yourself?" he asked.

I figured I already had my answer. "Just curious," I said. 'Thanks, Lieutenant."

"Wait a minute, March," he said. "Have you been nosing around?"

"Me?" I said innocently. "I've just been out soaking up some of this California atmosphere."

He had a short struggle with himself. "Look, March," he said finally, "I'll level with you. I think you're pretty much out of the woods. If you're talking about what I think you are, I noticed the scratches on Fancy Bradford's face. I didn't forget them. But he's got a damned good alibi, and he's beaten homicide raps before. I think we could prove she scratched him, but that doesn't prove he killed her. If Bradford did the killing, I'll get him—and I'll do it without any amateurs from Colorado mixing into it. Is that clear?"

"I'm just a guy on a vacation," I said. I started down the hall. "I'll see you around, Lieutenant."

"Yeah," he said heavily. "You will."

Outside, I took my time about getting started. When I finally pulled away from the curb, I was amused to see that there were two cars trailing me.

I stopped in town and went into a ten-cent store. When I came out I was carrying a package of children's modeling clay. I'd had the clerk leave it unwrapped in hopes that maybe the tails could see it. It would give them something to think about.

I went straight back to my bungalow at the hotel and took off my coat. I got the shoulder holster out of my suitcase and strapped it on. I picked up the .38 and slipped it in the holster. I then I put my coat back on. I started playing with the modeling clay and waiting.

I didn't have long to wait. It was only about five minutes before there was a knock on the door. "Come in," I said.

The door opened and they came in fast: Lance Harker and Barry Alfama. Both of them had their guns out as they stepped through the door.

"Make it easy on yourself," Lance Harker said. His voice

was tight and there was an eager look in his eyes. I was careful not to make any sudden moves.

The short guy was staring at my hands, "Look, Lance," he said. "The guy's making dolls. You think he's blown his oats?"

"It won't make any difference now," Lance said. He came across the room, walking carefully. He patted me again and found the gun. He slipped it in his pocket. "Let's go, March."

"Where?" I said.

"We're going to show you the sights," he said. He prodded me with the gun. "Move."

The three of us left the bungalow as chummy as an egg with three yolks. The guns vanished into their pockets as soon as we stepped outside, but Lance was walking so close to me I could still feel the gun barrel.

Out on the street we climbed into their car, Lance and me in the back, the short guy in front. The gun came back into the open as the car pulled away.

I couldn't twist around to see if my other tail was still on the job. I hoped he was, and let it go at that. Neither of Fancy's boys showed any desire to be chatty as we headed down Wilshire, so I let it ride. Their conversation was likely to be limited anyway.

It took us about forty minutes to reach the store on the Strip. When we parked, Lance prodded me with the gun again.

"Outside, sucker," he said.

I got out, and we went into the store. As we crossed the sidewalk, I caught a glimpse of someone jumping out of a car behind us and running into a drugstore. But I couldn't tell whether it meant anything for me or was just a guy with a headache.

We marched through the store and up to the office door. The short guy opened it and stepped inside. I hesitated, and Lance belted me lightly across the back of the neck with the gun. I stumbled into the doorjamb, then got my balance and walked inside. Lance followed me in and circled around to one side. Fancy Bradford sat behind the desk, looking at me. This time he wasn't grinning.

"This time he was loaded, boss," Lance said. He reached over and flipped back my coat to show the empty holster.

"If you wanted to see me," I said, "why didn't you just phone? I told you I don't like to be pushed around."

"You'll be pushed more," he said. "I thought I told you to keep your nose clean. The minute you were out of here, you started asking questions about me. Then you went running to the cops again."

"Just to get you a present," I said. I reached in my pocket and took out the watch. I tossed it to him. "I thought maybe you'd like this back."

Fancy looked at the watch and put it down on the desk. "Where'd you get it?"

"From the cops—without their permission. I thought you'd like it as a keepsake."

He pushed the watch with his finger. "What are you up to, March? You trying to frame me?"

"I don't have to frame you," I said. "You did it." I started to go over to sit down in the chair.

"Stay where you are," he said. "You ain't going nowhere. I

was willing to let you go, March, but you had to keep shoving. You're the only witness against me, and I'm going to make you wish the frame on you had stuck."

"The way you did with Sherry?" I asked.

"Not with the knife," he said. "I cut her throat because I didn't want any noise. Then the bitch had to scream. But we won't treat you that way. I don't want lousy cop blood all over my place."

"Why don't you just keep talking," I said, "and you could bore me to death. It would be the perfect murder."

"Let me work on him a little, boss," Lance said. He sounded eager, but I'd already guessed he loved his work. "He talks too smart."

"Go ahead," Fancy said, "but make it fast. The quicker we got a dead witness, the better I'll like it."

The tall gunman moved in on me. I watched him carefully. The barrel of his gun was a blue blur as he swung it at me. I tried to roll a little with it as it hit my jaw. But it still made my teeth ache and knocked me back a couple of steps. I felt a spurt of blood down my chin. I tried to take a quick look around.

Maybe the next one would do it. He was starting to enjoy himself. His eyes were getting a little feverish, and he licked his lips as he took another step toward me. He swung the gun again. It was meant for my eyes, but I ducked a little and it caught me on the forehead. I felt the gunsight scrape off another patch of skin. I didn't have to fake any staggering. The blow was hard enough to knock me all the way back. The edge of the chair smacked the back of my legs and I flopped into it. I was never so glad to sit down in my life.

"You see, boss?" Lance said thickly. "He's another guy that talks tough but is chicken when it comes to the real thing. ... Come on. Get up, I don't want to spoil the boss's good chair."

The room had stopped spinning and I could see him again. I took a good look.

"That would be tough," I said. I dropped my hand, then raised the derringer I'd hidden in the chair when I was there earlier. I pulled the trigger. The nastiness was suddenly gone from his face and there was blood in its place. It looked better that way.

I swiveled the gun and pulled the trigger again. The little guy had been lifting his own gun, but he suddenly dropped it and grabbed at his belly. I turned my attention to Fancy. He was fast, I'll say that much for him. He had a gun halfway out of the drawer in his desk. I put the third bullet in the desk about two inches in front of him.

"Drop it," I said. "I've got a fourth bullet in this, but I want to save you for that gas chamber."

He dropped the gun back in the drawer.

The door opened and Lieutenant Little came in. There were three county cops with him.

"Where the hell were you?" I said. "Did you have to stay out there playing patty-cake when that lug was beating me up?"

"We didn't want to interfere with your plan, and of course you neglected to tell me what it was," he said. He gave me a nasty grin. That's the thanks you get for helping a cop. "We heard Fancy confess he killed the girl, but we thought he might talk some more."

Fancy Bradford looked even sicker at that. "You couldn't have heard me," he said. "This is a soundproof room."

"It's soundproof when the door is closed," I told him. "But when I came in, I stuck a healthy wad of clay on the jamb so the door wouldn't close. I thought the Lieutenant was following—and you know how a cop is when he spots a partly open door. He's got to listen."

Lieutenant Little walked around and snapped a pair of cuffs on Fancy. "This is a pleasure," he said.

I stood up and mopped some of the blood off my face. "You ought to have enough now," I said. "I can identify him. You'll have the skin scrapings, and his confession. Then, there on his desk, is the watch he once gave Sherry."

The Lieutenant looked startled when he saw it. "Where'd that come from?" he asked. "That was in the lab."

"He must have lifted it when he was there this morning," I said. "The jury shouldn't find that hard to believe. He was afraid that would pin him to her even more. But, Lieutenant, you ought to put some burglar alarms around the station. Or hire a good cop to keep an eye on things. … I'll see you around."

"Don't bother," he said sourly. "The quicker you go back to Denver, the better I'll like it. We may work a little slower here, but we like it."

"Want me to leave right now?"

"No," he said. "You know damn well you can't. You'll have to appear for a hearing on these two stiffs. It was self-defense, but there'll have to be a hearing anyway. And you're a witness, don't forget."

"Then I'll see you around," I said with a grin as I left.

It was beginning to get dark when I reached my hotel again.

I was walking toward my bungalow, wondering about the one part of the puzzle that still bothered me.

"Hello," a voice said. "What happened to you yesterday?"

It was the other redhead—the one in the bikini. Now she was wearing a dress, but it only covered up; it didn't conceal. She was standing in the doorway of the bungalow next to mine—the one in between mine and the end bungalow, where I'd seen her the day before.

"Aren't you staying in that bungalow?" I asked, pointing to the end one.

She looked blank for a minute, then laughed. "I was just looking at that one to see if I liked it better than this. The maid had left the door open. Didn't I mention that?"

"No, you didn't," I said.

"You promised to come back and tell me about the scream," she said. "What happened?"

I looked to see if she was joking. She didn't seem to be. "I'm Milo March," I said.

She thought I was just introducing myself. "I'm Joyce Tallman," she said.

"Don't you ever read the newspapers?" I asked.

She shook her head. The red-gold hair danced on her bare shoulders. "Not when I'm on vacation," she said. "Did I miss something?"

I took a deep breath and let it out slowly. "Not very much," I said. "I'll tell you about it, if you'll join me in a drink."

"I'd love to," she said.

Later that night, I thought I heard another scream. Maybe it was only the wind in the palm trees, but it sounded like a woman. But I didn't bother to go out to investigate. There was one redhead in my room, and she was very much alive. I didn't see any point in going out and maybe ending up with another dead one.

3

The Hot Ice Blues

It was a nice day. The air was cool and crisp, with a tang to it that made you realize why so many people came to Denver for their health. I'd stayed home the night before, spinning a few records and then going to bed, so I was feeling clear-eyed and filled with the contentment of the pure in heart. If anyone had asked me, I would have staked my life there was nothing but peace and quiet ahead of me. I couldn't have been more mistaken.

I parked my car in the lot back of the Gilmore Building and took the elevator to the tenth floor, the office of Inter-World Insurance Service Corporation. I opened the door, went in, and then stopped to admire the scenery. Our receptionist is a girl with blue-black hair, peaches-and-cream skin, and the kind of figure that would make calculus an interesting hobby. I stopped in front of her desk and leaned over to get a better look at her peekaboo neckline. She cheated by pulling back. That was normal for her; she had the best bait in the world, but she was throwing everything back in until she caught a guy with a proposal instead of a proposition.

"Not fair," I said, shaking a finger at her. "How do you expect me to admire your beauty properly if you keep backing off?"

"It's not the admiration I mind," she said. "It's the teeth marks I want to avoid. Milo, are you drunk again?"

I shook my head truthfully. "It's just my new brandy-flavored toothpaste—March's answer to all the chlorophyll products. What awaits my special talents this morning?"

"Nothing, so far as I know," she said. "There's somebody in with him, but I don't know if it means anything."

"Him" was Niels Bancroft, owner and president of Inter-World, who sat in his private office just beyond a handsome oak door, and who spent most of his time trying to figure out ways of keeping me busy. He usually succeeded.

"I refuse to be intimidated," I said airily, "by the thought of work. It's too nice a day. If you want me, I'll be in my office, communing with nature."

"Spelled b-r-a-n-d-y?" she asked sweetly.

"Bluenose!" I snapped and went on into my cubicle. It had a frosted glass door with my name—*Milo March*—on it in small black letters. You had only to compare it with the other doors in the place to know who did the work around Inter-World. Inside there was a hat rack, a filing cabinet, a chair, and a desk. All of them were battered from much use. I hung up my hat and sat in the chair.

I looked out the window. It still was a nice day, but all I could see were a bunch of office windows and a lot of girls busily punching typewriters, adding machines, and comptometers. It was too depressing to watch all that work, so I opened a desk drawer and took out my favorite office equipment—a bottle of brandy. I took a small one, just so I'd know the day was officially started.

It was about ten minutes later that my phone rang. It was Peaches-and-Cream.

"He wants to see you," she said. "He's using his VIP voice."

That meant Niels had asked to have "Mr. March" come in, instead of calling me "that S.O.B.," as he usually did. Which, in turn, meant that he was trying to impress whoever was in with him. Niels Bancroft trying to impress someone was about as nauseating a spectacle as anyone could wish to see.

I took another drink and left my office. I knew Niels liked to have everyone knock at his office door when he had visitors, but I thought, to hell with it! I opened his door and went in.

Niels is a big man who looks like an ex-pug. His hair is gray, and there are gray tufts thrusting out of his ears. He chain-smokes, sticking half the cigarette in his mouth, and lights his cigarettes with old-fashioned kitchen matches. He wears $200 suits. Usually his coat is over the back of his chair and his tie looks as if it has just gone through a wrestling match, but on this day he was wearing his coat and was still letting the tie choke him.

As soon as I'd taken in the details, I looked around to see the reason. He sat in the chair beside Niels's desk, looking like television's dream of the perfect executive. Everything he wore was neat, expensive, and unruffled. He wasn't any older than I am, maybe about thirty-five, but the expression on his face was all laced up as if he were wearing a corset on his brain. His face was too tanned, his teeth too white, and his eyes too blue—if you know what I mean. I decided right them that I didn't like him and that it probably would be mutual.

"Mr. Hanley," Niels said, using his country-club voice,

"this is Milo March, who handles most of our investigations. I'm sure you're familiar with his work even though you've never met him before. Milo, this is Mr. Hanley, of Providential Insurance." He accented the last two words, and I began to understand part of it. Providential was one of the biggest companies in the country and gave us at least a third of our business.

"Just call me Jerry," the Perfect Executive said heartily. He stood up. "I certainly am familiar with Milo's work. I'm sure we'll get along splendidly."

He reached out and shook my hand. He had a manly handshake—the kind where you remember him every time you try to move a finger for two weeks. When I finally got my hand back, I started to count my fingers, but Niels frowned so heavily that I gave up.

"Ummm," I said, figuring that didn't commit me to anything.

"Mr. Hanley will be sharing your office for a few days," Niels said. His voice indicated that I should exhibit childish glee over this bit of information.

It had been so successful the first time, I tried it again. "Ummm," I said.

Niels cleared his throat louder than usual. "Mr. Hanley," he said, "is here on a matter which is very important to his company—and to us. I've just been telling him that we will, of course, cooperate to the fullest."

"Selling insurance?" I asked brightly, looking at Mr. Hanley.

"Mr. Hanley," Niels said hastily, "is a vice-president of Providential. He's in charge of all their investigations. Now

I'd like him to tell you himself the reason he's here in Denver."

"That might help," I admitted.

Hanley picked up a briefcase from the floor. It was a

vice-president-type briefcase, with gold initials. He opened it and took out a neat sheaf of papers. He didn't bother to look at them, but he did tap them with one manicured fingernail. It was a vice-president-type gesture.

"We," he said, tapping for each word, "have been taking a beating recently with jewel thefts. Not only us; as a matter of fact, we are cooperating with other companies on this, and on this trip I am representing Great Northern as well as my own company. I believe that Great Northern is also one of your clients."

Niels nodded. Hanley went on: "We believe we are dealing with a very clever gang of jewel thieves, probably no more two or three persons. They have been working west of here—Los Angeles, San Francisco, and then Reno. In Reno, I received a tip that they were heading for Denver. This time I am hoping to catch them in the act."

"We will," Niels said emphatically.

"Efficiency and organization will do it," Hanley said. "They have shown an ability for picking out large policyholders. I've made a list of those in Denver which might be large enough to attract the thieves. There are fifteen of them, covered by Great Northern and ourselves. I intend to investigate thoroughly every one of these immediately. With the aid of that information and the cooperation of the local police, I feel sure we can prevent any loss on policies in this area."

"Wouldn't it be simpler," I asked, "to warn all the policyholders that the gang is supposed to be heading this way, and ask them to stick their family jewels in a safe-deposit box until the storm blows over?"

He looked at me as if I'd said a dirty word. "So they'd go on to the next city? We can't run around asking everyone to lock up their jewels all the time. This way, if we're on our toes, we'll catch them and that will put an end to it."

"How much did they get so far?" I asked.

"Close to five million out of the three cities," he said. "None of it has been fenced yet, so we're guessing they have some scheme for fencing it that will bring them more than the usual ten percent."

"Even ten percent of five million isn't bad," I said. "Maybe they'll try to make a deal with you."

"I wish they would. Right now we'd be glad to pay a million dollars for the return of the jewels. But there hasn't been a feeler yet."

"Well, we'll stop them here," Niels declared. "You go ahead, Mr. Hanley, and make yourself comfortable in Milo's office. Milo will be in shortly. I've got to clean up a few points with him and then he'll be yours."

Hanley nodded, gathered up his briefcase, and walked out. Niels waited until the door closed, then turned to me. There was an angry glint in his eye.

"You got any ideas about not cooperating with Hanley," he told me, "you'd better get rid of them. And try to act a little more as if this was a place of business. No more brandy nipping in your office."

"Why don't you relax?" I said. "Unfasten your tie before you start turning blue."

He glared at me. "I'm warning you, Milo—"

"I got a hunch about that guy," I interrupted. "You want to

hear it? Hanley may be a vice-president in charge of investigations, but for my money he's always been under the desk. He's going to spend all his time working out graphs and laying out programs, and while he's doing it the thieves could walk off with the whole city of Denver. I'm not going to be turned into a clerk, even for a vice-president. Especially a clerk who can't drink anything but water."

"You'll work with him," Niels said grimly, "or you'll find yourself picking up garbage for the city."

"What makes you think that would be any different from this job?" I asked him. I turned and left before he could think of an answer.

Back in my own office, I found Hanley had already taken over my chair and desk. I got one of the chairs from the reception room and planted it in front of the desk. Then I went around beside him, excused myself politely, and opened the drawer to get my bottle of brandy.

"Care for a small portion?" I asked him, waving the bottle in his face.

He looked like somebody's maiden aunt being given a guided tour of the red-light district. "I never drink during business hours," he said. "It impairs efficiency."

"Speak for yourself," I said cheerfully. I took a drink and set the bottle on the edge of the desk. "Now, then—the game's afoot, eh?"*

He didn't like that either, but he let it pass. After that he kept me so damn busy I didn't get a chance for any more cracks.

---

* Milo is probably quoting from a story (or film) in which Sherlock Holmes wakes Dr. Watson with a quote from Shakespeare: "Come, Watson, come. The game is afoot."

I'd been right about him. He already had all kinds of graphs, and a city map with the location of the fifteen policyholders carefully marked out. Right away he started going out and seeing all of them, while he put me to work making more graphs out of the information he collected. We practically knew what time everyone went to the bathroom.

But that was only the beginning. He went down to see Lieutenant Blair Wayne, who headed the Burglary Squad, and threw his weight around. The Lieutenant put two men on night duty at each of the fifteen houses. Then Hanley arranged for the policyholders to notify us any evening they were going out, and the Lieutenant agreed to double the men in such cases. To top it off, he arranged with somebody down at headquarters for the two of us to ride in the two prowl cars that covered most of the Gold Coast at night.

I'd never worked so hard in my life. I didn't even have time for drinking. Before Hanley showed up, I used to get to the office at maybe ten in the morning. When things were slow, I left by four. Now I had to be there at nine. I slaved over paperwork until six, then grabbed a quick bite, hopped into a prowl car, and rode around with two disgusted cops until two in the morning. Then Hanley reluctantly let me go home and get some sleep.

With all that careful preparation, you could guess what would happen. That's right. On the third night, somebody broke into the home of Mr. and Mrs. Jay Grammer and made off with all of Mrs. Grammer's ice—a hundred grand worth.

No, nothing went wrong. Everything was carried out as planned, but the burglars refused to cooperate. Mr. and Mrs.

ILLUSTRATED BY STAN DRAKE

Grammer were out for a night on the town. There were two cops in front of the house and two more in the back. One prowl car passed along the front street several times, and I guess the other one passed along the back just as often. Nobody saw anything wrong, but when the Grammers came home, the baubles were gone. The thieves had inconsiderately gone in through a side window, then out the same way, and the detectives had seen nothing.

The next night it was the home of Mr. and Mrs. Robert Ardmore, ten blocks away from where the Grammers lived. This time the take was insured at a hundred and twenty-five thousand. And the following night it was the home of Mr. and Mrs. Sanford Hopkins, who lived right next door to the Grammers. The take was worth only seventy-five thousand. The picayuneness of the amount seemed to upset Mrs. Hopkins more than anything else.

Everybody was pretty much in a tizzy. Lieutenant Blair Wayne was beginning to feel like a patsy. It was bad enough for him anytime there were successful robberies, but with them being pulled off right under his nose, the newspapers were beginning to act as if he needed a Seeing Eye dog. Irate citizens were screaming at him, and our Mr. Hanley was also giving him the works. Hanley seemed to think Wayne was wasting time when he insisted on shaking down all the local boys he could lay his hands on, instead of looking only for the mysterious strangers who had apparently come from Reno.

Hanley was also jumping all over me. At times, he seemed to think that if I'd only make a dozen more graphs, the names of the heist boys might suddenly appear between the lines. Spirit writing, probably.

"Look at them!" he shouted the day after the third robbery. He had brightly colored pins stuck in the map at the location of the three homes. "What kind of system are they using to pick out victims? That's our answer, March. All we've got to do is find the *pattern;* then we can grab them at the next job."

"Ummm," I said. That was about the extent of my end of the conversation with Mr. Hanley.

"We've got to find the *pattern*," he said, thumping one fist into his other hand. "We've got to get on the ball, March, got to pressure-cook this thing. Do you realize they've already taken over two hundred thousand dollars—"

I think something snapped in me. I distinctly heard a click. "Just a minute," I said solemnly. "If we're going to pressure-cook this, I think I need a drink of water. I'll be right back."

I gave him a sign to show that I was about to get on the ball, and walked out of the office. I stopped by the reception desk and looked down at Peaches-and-Cream.

"Sweetheart," I said, "if our Mr. Hanley should happen to get worried about my absence, you tell him I just worked out a quick graph on myself and discovered I'm about due for a nervous breakdown. Tell him I've gone out to pressure-cook it."

She giggled. "Milo, you're sober," she said accusingly.

I hung my head in shame and left the office. Downstairs, I climbed into my car and went home. When I got there, I called up the phone company and told them I was going on vacation and wanted my phone disconnected. Then I double-locked the door, took a good stiff drink of brandy, and went to bed. I slept the sleep of the just.

It was five o'clock in the afternoon when I awoke. I brewed some coffee, laced it with brandy, and sat down for the first relaxed minute I'd had in almost a week. By the time I'd finished, I almost stopped seeing graphs in front of my eyes.

I poured myself some more brandy and got into my thinking position. It was a pleasure.

A couple of hours later I left the apartment. I stopped in a little restaurant and had something to eat. Then I drove downtown, to a section of Denver that never had to worry about jewelry losses, parked in front of a battered old rooming house, and went in. This was where a little junkie named Whistles Naylor lived. For the price of a heroin fix, he'd tell anything he knew. Everybody knew this, and no one ever really took him into confidence, but he still managed to pick up odds and ends, so he often came in handy. No one had any use for Whistles, but I liked him. He was a long way past rehabilitation; it was too late for Whistles to do anything but stay in the heroin fog he'd built for himself. I used to stop by and slip him a few bucks every week or so whether I wanted information or not.

I walked upstairs and stopped in front of his door. After a minute, I heard a rustling inside, like that of mice. Whistles was home. I knocked on the door.

"Who is it?" he asked. His voice was a high-pitched whine, but it barely reached through the door. Constant fear had put a permanent damper on his voice the fear of being without heroin and the fear that someday he'd talk about the wrong thing.

"Milo March," I said.

After a minute he opened the door, just wide enough for me to sidle in. His tiny room was lit by a single blue bulb. He'd once explained to me that the blue light was better; when he was loaded, bright lights hurt his eyes.

Whistles was a small man with a ratlike face the color of a fish's belly. His clothes had come from the Salvation Army and were at least three sizes too large. The room was filled with the pungent odor of unwashed linen and narcotics.

"Gee, Milo," he said, "I thought maybe you'd be around." The muscles in his face were twitching slightly. I knew the signs. Whistles needed a shot. "I read about somebody heisting all the flash, and I figured you'd be around."

"You know something about it?" I asked. I lit a cigarette and puffed on it rapidly. The smoke helped the air a little, but not much.

He shook his head and his face twitched still more. "I ain't heard nothing," he said regretfully. "I was tryin' to remember, but I ain't thinking no good." He looked at me hopefully.

"You'll get a fix," I told him. "Think some more, Whistles. Anybody around with more money than usual? Maybe spending more than he usually does?"

His face wrinkled with effort. "Frankie Brand," he said finally. "He was buyin' the boys drinks last night in Three Fingers' place. Frankie don't buy drinks usually, unless he's just pulled a job." From his tone, I knew that Whistles considered it a long shot.

"Maybe," I said. "What about strangers, Whistles? You heard anything about any strangers being in town?"

He shook his head.

"Maybe it's Frankie, then," I said. "You think you could find out a little more from Frankie himself?"

I could see fear and need struggling in his face. I hated

like hell to see it. I knew as well as Whistles did that it was dangerous for him to start asking anyone questions.

"Maybe," he said finally. "I guess I could do it, Milo … if I only had a needle—"

I took ten dollars out of my pocket and handed it to him. "There'll be more after you've picked up something," I said. "I'll meet you back here."

He nodded. I left the room and went downstairs, got into my car, and drove around the block. When Whistles came scurrying out of the room, I followed him on foot.

Whistles went into another rooming house a few blocks away. I knew he was making his contact, so I stayed down on the street. In about ten minutes he appeared again. This time he was walking with more confidence and didn't seem worried about anyone following him. He'd had his needle-ful of courage.

A few blocks away, he turned and went into a bar. This was the place owned by a guy known as Three Fingers. At some time or other you could find almost every Denver criminal there. Half the illegal deals of the city were made in the rooms back of the bar.

There was no way of peering in since the windows were so dirty you couldn't see through them, so I walked around the block and then went inside. I wanted to keep an eye on Whistles, not because I didn't trust him but because I didn't want to see him killed, and I knew he was treading on thin ice.

The bar was crowded. The lights were pretty dim, but I soon spotted Whistles. He was at the far end of the bar, talking to a guy I'd never seen before—a big, tough-looking guy, well dressed, with the bulge under his coat that was practically a sartorial necessity in Three Fingers's place.

I slid into an empty place at the bar where I could keep an eye on Whistles in the mirror. I drew a number of quick looks, but nobody seemed to know me, so nothing happened. The men who stood near me stopped talking. The bartender looked me over, but agreed to serve me a shot of straight brandy. It wasn't very good brandy, but then I hadn't expected it to be.

I was on my third brandy when I saw Whistles suddenly turn and walk stiffly away from the bar. The big, tough-looking guy went with him. They headed for the men's room, walking close together—too close. And both of them had unfinished drinks on the bar. I didn't like the looks of it. I waited until they'd gone through the door. Then I set my glass down and drifted casually in the same direction. No one was looking at me, but I knew that everyone at the bar was aware of my movements. And the bartender was strolling down toward the end of the bar just as casually.

He came around the end of the bar and met me just before I reached the door.

"Going somewhere?" he asked. One hand was behind his back, but I had a good idea what was in it.

"Yeah," I said.

"Better wait," he said. He was a big guy with a face that had been worked over so many times it no longer looked like a face. "Somebody is in there already."

"Can't wait," I said. "It looks big enough to hold all of us."

"What's your hurry, chum?" he asked. He was still being pleasant.

"That's my business," I told him.

"I could make it mine."

I shook my head. "You wouldn't like it. The hours are too long and you meet the wrong class of people."

"Wise guy!" he said. His voice lost its smoothness. "Wait."

I put a cigarette in my mouth and reached for a match. Only I came out with my gun instead. I shoved it up against his belly, just trying it for size.

"Where I come from" I said, "bartenders are supposed to tend bar. Go mix yourself a drink while you can still hold it."

I could see the muscles quivering under his shirt, but he didn't let it go beyond that. He turned and walked back toward the bar, his fingers gripping the short bat, so hard the knuckles were white. I turned and went into the men's room, fast.

Whistles was down on the floor and the big guy had one fist knotted in his hair. The other fist was just drawn back to strike.

"What the—" he said, starting to turn.

He never made it. I slapped the gun barrel across his jaw as he turned, and he went down, his head bouncing on the tile floor.

"Milo—" Whistles started to gasp.

"Don't talk now," I said. I looked around. There was an open window at the back of the men's room. "Go out the window and wait for me in your room. Jump."

He jumped. He went out through the window like a scared rabbit. I bent over the boy on the floor. He would have a couple of lumps on his head, but that was all. I went through his pockets. It was practically a dry run. He had a driver's license identifying him as Frank Brand. There was a gun and a sap in his pocket. And a little more than $9,000 in cash. That was all.

I dragged him into one of the cubicles and propped him up. I went to the door and opened it just enough to look out. There was a row of men at the bar, none of them talking and all of them watching that door the way a cat watches a mouse hole.

To hell with dignity! I went out by the window, too.

Whistles had recovered most of his courage by the time I reached his room, but he was still worried.

"Gee, Milo," he said, "Frankie might've knocked me off if you hadn't got there. You think he'll come here?"

"Not for a few minutes," I said, "and we'll take care of that. What happened?"

"We was just talkin' and I guess he suddenly got the idea I was asking too many questions. He was trying to find out who put me up to it."

"Did you get anything?"

"Not much." Whistles said. "He's been pulling some jobs, but he didn't say what kind. He did say that the stuff was being fenced right away and he was gettin' his cut in cash."

It was a long shot, but it seemed to add up. Stolen jewels normally bring about ten percent of their value when they're fenced. So far, the jewels lifted in Denver added up to about $200,000. Ten percent of that would be $20,000. And half of that would be $10,000. Frankie Brand had a little more than $9,000 in his pockets when I searched him. The only thing against it as a good guess was that Lieutenant Wayne had sworn that none of the jewelry had been fenced.

Anyway, that was all Whistles was going to be able to get for me. And Whistles was apt to be hot for a few days. I took him out of there. On the way, I gave him some more money and stopped so he could get himself a supply of H. Then I took him on to another rooming house and got him a room under my name. He promised me he'd stay there, and I was pretty sure he would—he had enough heroin to keep him fog-happy for several days.

I headed back uptown and stopped in at one of my favorite bars, where the brandy was good enough to wash away the taste left in my mouth by the stuff I'd bought in Three Fingers's bar. Not having any idea of the next step, I proceeded to tie one on. And halfway through, just when I was beginning to feel like I was on cloud nine, I got myself an idea. It was a pretty one.

I stopped off at the Gilmore Building and used my key to get into the office. I messed around among the records for a while, ignoring all the fancy stuff added by Hanley, and finally found our list of Great Northern and Providential clients. I made a copy and stuck it in my pocket. Then I picked up the phone and called Niels at home.

"Milo!" he bellowed when he recognized my voice. "You're fi—"

"You can't fire me," I said, "because I quit this morning."

"Don't talk back to me," he started again.

"Niels," I said, "get it through your thick head. I quit this morning because I won't have a square like that Hanley shoved off on me. I've got a couple of thousand saved up—

enough to take me to New York, where I figure I won't have too much trouble getting a job with one of the other companies. I just called to say goodbye."

That got him. He knew it was true that I wouldn't have any trouble getting a job in New York.

"Now, wait a minute, Milo," he said. "Don't go off half-cocked. You know you like it in Denver. You wouldn't be happy in New York. I've always treated you right, haven't I?"

"Until this time," I said. I waited a couple of beats. "I'll stay on one condition, Niels."

"What?"

"That I don't have to come into the office or have anything to do with Hanley until this is over."

"Look, Milo, I can't do that. Great Northern and Providential represent at least half of our business. We have to handle Hanley with kid gloves."

"*You* have to," I said. "If we cleaned up this series of thefts. Great Northern and Providential wouldn't care if we kicked all their vice-presidents in the teeth. Isn't that so?"

"Y-yes."

"Then take your choice. I'll stay under the conditions I just stated. Otherwise, I'm catching the first plane out in the morning."

"Do you think you can clear up the thefts, working independently of Hanley?" he asked.

"Have I ever fallen down on a job?" I asked him.

"No." I could hear him taking a deep breath. "All right, Milo. But heaven help me if you don't come up with the answer, and if Hanley ever finds out what I've done."

"He'll be so busy making graphs, he'll never notice," I said. "Pour yourself a stiff drink and forget about it." I replaced the receiver and left the office. I had a couple more drinks in a bar around the corner. Then, feeling no pain, I went home and went to bed.

I heard on the radio the next morning that there'd been another robbery the night before: more jewels. The home of Mr. and Mrs. Cranston had been entered, despite a heavy police guard, and jewels worth $150,000 had been taken.

After breakfast, I went down to police headquarters. I figured Hanley would be busy at the office with his figures.

I found Blair Wayne in his office, looking as if he hadn't slept for a week.

"And happy diamonds to you, too," I said, sticking my head in.

He glared at me. "Drop dead." He said. "I got enough troubles, any way you look at it, but right now I wish I'd never heard of insurance companies or the people who work for them. The next insurance guy who comes to Denver is going to get run right out of town."

"Hanley?" I asked.

"Your friend Hanley," he said. "The more I let myself get talked into cooperating, the more trouble I get myself into. You know where I was last night, Milo?"

"At the opera?"

"I was riding in a prowl car with Hanley and two cops. We didn't do a damn thing but ride around and around the block on which the Cranston house is, and that's what we were doing when somebody walked off with the family jewels."

"Ringside seat," I said, grinning.

"Sure, only I didn't see anything. And you know what the papers are making out of that. This happens a couple more times and I'll be back pounding a beat myself! I've already had a talk with the Commissioner this morning, and I'll bet that most of the phone insulation is burned to a crisp. Now what the hell do you want?"

"I wanted to ask a question." I said. "Hanley mentioned that you said none of the stuff was being fenced. That right?"

"None of it is being fenced in Denver," he said. "I'll stake my job on that. Furthermore, while your friend Hanley keeps yapping about a slick jewel ring invading us from Reno, I can't find any evidence of any strangers in town. And even though your friend Hanley told me I was wasting my time, I shook down all the local boys without turning up a thing."

"Stop calling him my friend," I said. "He's a vice-president, and so he's nobody's friend. So long, Lieutenant—I'll see you at the unemployment office." I ducked the pencil he threw at me and left.

I drove downtown and paid a short visit to Whistles. After that, I stopped off to see a friend of his. Then I drove back uptown to see if I could get anywhere on a small idea that was buzzing around in my head.

My first stop was the Dixie Record Shop. The only reason I went there was that I wanted to try to stick to something I knew, and there had been a period when I was really digging it. I cornered the guy who runs the record shop and showed him a list with four names on it.

"Any of these customers of yours?" I asked him.

He pointed to one of the names. "She is," he said. "In fact, I've got an order I'm delivering to her today."

"Hold it until I get back," I said. I didn't run into that kind of luck every day and I wanted to latch on to it. I drove home to my apartment and scrounged around in one of the closets. It was filled with records. I picked out several that I wanted and went back down to the car.

I left the rest of them in the car and took one of the records into the shop with me. I handed it to him. He took one look at it and whistled.

"You want to sell this?" he asked.

I shook my head. "I want you to slip that in with the records you're sending her."

He looked doubtful. "I don't know if I can do that, Milo."

"It's legal," I said. "You're not doing anything wrong. Just slip it in with the other records, and then forget all about it. It's not only legal, but you'll be doing the lady a favor."

He was still doubtful, but he finally agreed to it. I went back out and sat in my car until I saw his delivery boy leave. Then I went for some lunch.

An hour later, I entered one of Denver's most expensive apartment houses. I had the rest of the records under my arm. I still needed a little luck on this try. If I didn't get it, I'd have to work out another approach with one of the other names on the list.

I got a couple of surprises when I knocked on the apartment door. It was opened by someone who quite obviously wasn't the maid or butler I was expecting. That made it easier. The second surprise was even nicer. I'd expected at least a middle-aged woman; the one who answered the door was strictly a chick. Long red hair curling down around her shoulders; a dream face with green eyes and full red lips. She was wearing a housecoat that must have come from Paris, and it couldn't have come to a better place. She was really stacked.

"Yes?" she said. There was a note of amusement in her voice, as though she had a good idea what I was thinking.

"Sorry," I said, with a grin which meant I wasn't. "I'm looking for Miss Linda Leyton."

"I'm Linda Leyton."

"You just got a delivery of platters from the Dixie Record Shop?"

She nodded, looking puzzled.

"I'm sorry to bother you," I said, "but I was in there when Joe was making up your order, and I think a record of mine got mixed in with the ones he was sending to you."

She smiled. "Come in," she said. "I haven't opened the records yet. We'll look."

She held the door open and I went in. The package from the Dixie Record Shop was on the coffee table. She went directly to it.

"What was your record?" she asked.

" 'Georgia Bo,' " I said—and held my breath waiting for a reaction.

I got it, in the way she looked at me. "What recording of it?" she asked.

"Louis Armstrong and His Hot Five." I said. I watched her closely. "Besides Louis, there was Kid Ory on trombone, Johnny Dodds on clarinet, Lil Hardin Armstrong on piano—"

"—And Johnny St. Cyr on banjo," she finished for me. I was in. She had that gone look on her face that only a real jazz addict would get at the mention of those names. I noticed her hands shook a little as she unwrapped the package. Then she had the record in her hands.

"I know all about this," she said, "but I've never heard it. Would you mind if I played it once, Mr.—"

"Milo March," I said. "Go ahead,"

She put the record on her player and we sat listening. It wasn't one of Louis's best records, but it was pretty good and it was rare. She sighed heavily when it finished.

"I've got some other platters here," I said when she went to take it off. "I've got some by Louis's second Hot Five. With 'Fatha' Hines on piano, Fred Robinson on trombone, Jimmy Strong on clarinet, Mancy Cara on banjo, and Zutty Single-ton on drums. I got 'West End Blues,' 'Fireworks,' 'Sugarfoot Strut,' and 'Squeeze Me.' Then I got Don Redman's record-ing of 'Chant of the Weed' and 'Shakin' the African.' And an Okeh waxing of 'That's How I Feel Today' and 'Six or Seven Times' by the Little Chocolate Dandies, with Rex Stewart, J.C. Higginbotham, Don Redman, Benny Carter, Coleman Hawkins, and Fats Waller. And I got 'Black Bottom Stomp' and 'Doctor Jazz' by Jelly Roll Morton's Red Hot Peppers. Then, let's see, here's Bessie Smith's 'Empty Bed Blues' and 'Shim-Me-Sha-Wabble' by the Original Wolverines." It was like walking into the White House and announcing that I had the hydrogen bomb in my pocket.

She laughed. "Man, you're crazy," she said.

"Real gone," I admitted. "Want to hear them?"

"Try to stop me," she challenged.

By the time we'd finished playing those records, we were old friends. Music will do that for you. Then she started bringing out her own records. She didn't have some of the old Dixie items that I had, but she had a lot of things I was missing. She had a collection of Ellington that even the Duke might have envied. She started feeding them into the machine. It was great.

When we got hungry, we sent out for sandwiches and beer and kept on playing records. It was so much fun I almost forgot that I'd arranged this with the idea of doing some work. But once, when she left me alone for a few minutes, I tore myself away from the music and went prowling around the apartment.

I was still in luck. In the bedroom, I found a jewel box containing a jade necklace. I knew it was only a part of her collection, but it was the most valuable part. I had a camera in my pocket, one that was small enough to fit in my hand. I got several good shots of the necklace and the box and made it back to the music before she showed. Then I went back to enjoying myself. It wasn't hard.

It was late when we finally broke it up. We both had a real music jag on and she slipped her hand in mine as she walked me to the door.

"It's been real cool," I said. "Shall we do it again?"

She nodded.

"As soon as we run through your collection, we can go over and start on mine," I said. "That ought to keep us in business for a while."

She laughed, "Then start all over again."

"Good," I said again, and left. I was feeling so good I even waved to the cop who was downstairs watching the front of the apartment house. That's how democratic I felt.

It was already well past midnight. I drove over to the Gilmore Building and went into the office again. I dug out the Linda Leyton file and started through it. Every time anyone has jewelry insured, the file not only includes a pretty thorough investigation on the person, but carries a complete description of all the pieces of jewelry insured. I wasted little time on personal curiosity. Linda Leyton was twenty-six years old and she'd never been married. She had jewelry worth $50,000, the jade necklace representing half of that. She'd also inherited a steady income, although she could not be called extremely wealthy. Finally I got down to the description of the necklace, which I copied. Then I went home.

I'd arranged my bathroom in my apartment so I could use it as a darkroom. I developed the pictures I'd taken and ran off several prints. When they were dry, I got back in my car and went downtown to visit Whistles's friend. He was in the kind of business where he was still available at three in the morning. After that I went home and to bed. I dreamed about a redheaded girl who could play the trumpet like Louis Armstrong.

When I woke it was midmorning. I had some coffee and then went downstairs. I called the phone company and told them I was back from my vacation and they could connect my phone again. Then I called Lieutenant Blair Wayne.

"How are we doing?" I asked.

"Great," he said heavily. "Why don't you try reading the morning papers instead of calling headquarters for your daily news bulletin?"

"You mean there was another one last night?"

"Bright boy!" he said. "Another seventy-five grand—from the Reese family. Mrs. Reese, by the way, is a cousin of the Commissioner. You know anybody who wants a slightly shopworn lieutenant of police?"

"Where were you when this happened?" I asked.

"Riding around the block with your friend Hanley and two cops—where else?" he said bitterly. "Only the newspapers called it pleasure-riding on the taxpayers money. Milo, haven't I always been your friend?"

"Sure."

"Haven't I always cooperated with you?"

"Yeah."

"Then do me a favor," he said. "Get that guy Hanley off my neck. He's practically running the department. I can't make a move without him breathing over my shoulder and uttering dire threats about what will happen if I don't clean this right up."

"Why don't you throw him in the cooler for obstructing justice or illegal parking or something?"

"You're behind the times, boy," he said. "Mr. Hanley went to see the mayor the first day. He showed that the two companies he's representing own umpteen millions of dollars of real estate in Denver, which entitles them to umpteen million kinds of cooperation. Mr. Hanley possesses a nice shiny badge as a special investigator for the D.A., and everybody, including the Commissioner, keeps telling me to be nice to him."

"Why not slip some poison in his coffee?" I suggested.

"I'm afraid my colleague Lieutenant Malikoff wouldn't approve. Now, if *you'd* care to make a slight sacrifice on behalf of the police—"

"Sorry," I said, "my astrologer told me not to commit murder while Venus is in the shadow of Mars. Some other time, perhaps."

"Oh, well!" He gave a mock sigh. "Milo, why were you consorting with a potential victim last night?"

"Me?" I said.

"You. And Miss Linda Leyton. You entered her apartment yesterday at two twenty-seven and left last night at twelve-fifteen. Is this the way you cooperate with me, not to mention your Mr. Hanley?"

"Oh, that," I said lightly. "I didn't even realize that Miss Leyton was one of the policyholders. This was purely a personal matter, Blair. We were listening to jazz records."

"Yeah?" he said. I could tell he didn't believe a word of it. "All I've got to say, Milo, is you picked a hell of a time to start developing your love life."

I just killed time for the rest of the day. That night I went up to see Linda Leyton again. We sat around listening to records. I didn't have any chores to do; all I did was listen to real groovy music and look at a beautiful woman.

The next day wasn't much different. I didn't bother to call anybody. The papers reported that there'd been another robbery, and there was a long editorial about the inefficiency of the police department and how nobody's property was safe. I hung around the house, caught up on some of my brandy drinking, and ignored the telephone whenever it squawked to life.

That evening I stopped by to see Whistles's friend again, and then I went up to Linda's apartment. That night we finished going through her collection of platters and even went back and played some of the first ones over. This time I got the chance to go in and take another look at her jade necklace. It was a pretty hunk of stuff. I made sure that I hadn't left any fingerprints, and went back to the music.

When I left that night, we made a date for Linda to come to my place the next night so we could start working through my records. I said I'd pick her up about seven, and I started to leave. Then something happened that wasn't in the script. I hadn't planned anything like that, but suddenly she was in my arms and her mouth was pressing against mine.

The next day was just another day, except that I found myself thinking more about Linda than about jewelry and insurance. There'd been still another robbery the night before—this made the sixth straight night that somebody had lost her pretties—but I didn't even care very much. I figured it would soon be over, but I started something else that wouldn't; at least, I hoped it wouldn't.

At seven that night, I stopped by the apartment to pick up Linda. I noticed there were more detectives around the building than usual, which meant Linda must have notified the police she was going out. That had been the only weak link in my idea; I hadn't been sure she'd do that. As soon as I saw the detectives, I stopped worrying and gave myself over to enjoying the evening.

We had dinner out, in a little place that featured a five-piece combo, which played jazz just good enough to whet or appetites. Then we went to my apartment. I'd spent the day, as soon as the cleaning woman had finished making the place presentable, in digging old records out of the closet and arranging them so I could get to the choice items.

I made some drinks and then we got down to serious business. I'd forgotten myself how much time and money I'd once put in on jazz. When I'd started digging out the platters in my closet, I discovered I had enough to go into business.

There were two funny things about that evening which most people would find hard to believe. This was the night I figured would start cracking the jewelry heists, but I never thought about jewels or good old Inter-World once. Secondly, I spent about six hours alone in my apartment with a beautiful redhead and we didn't even hold hands. We were getting to be old friends just by listening to music.

It was almost three in the morning when I took her home. I could see by the detectives that, so far as they were concerned, not a thing had happened. I took Linda upstairs, kissed her once, and went back down to the street.

I didn't feel like hanging around talking to cops, so I headed for my car. But before I could start, a patrol car pulled along side of me.

"Pretty soft," a voice said. It was Wayne, in the back of the cruiser. "How does it feel to be a playboy while the rest of us are working?"

"Great," I said, and meant it.

"Is that March?" another voice demanded. It was Hanley, the vice-presidents' vice-president. He was beginning to look a little worn, but he was still the perfect tired man of distinction. "I'm glad we ran into you, March. I just want to tell you that you'll never get another insurance job as long as you live. Any man who'll run out in the middle of a job—"

"Why, Jerry, old man," I said, "you misunderstand me. I'm just doing a little pressure-cooking, getting on the ball, you know."

I drove off before he could answer.

I was up early the next morning. I had some coffee and drove straight down to headquarters to find out how I was doing. I didn't even bother to pick up a paper.

It turned out I was doing better than I had expected. Wayne was in his office, all right, looking as though he hadn't been to bed at all; but he wasn't alone. Another old friend of mine was with him: Lieutenant Murray Malikoff of Homicide. At first, I thought it was just a coincidence.

"Don't tell me that Miss Leyton was robbed last night?" I said as I stopped in the doorway.

The two cops looked at each other. "What's his angle in this?" Malikoff growled.

"I'm not sure," Wayne said. "He claims he's not doing anything but playing around. But last night he was out with the Leyton girl. In fact, he's been with her every night for three nights. And never bothered to tell her that he's an insurance investigator. Now he comes galloping in here to find out about the Leyton robbery—and this one isn't in the papers yet."

Maybe I should have picked up a paper. I looked at them and thought fast. "It figured," I said. "The list is narrowing down, and she was away last night; I just guessed that maybe they'd hit there last night."

"Some little guesser," Wayne said sourly. "Maybe you can also make a guess about the robber we got this morning?"

That surprised me, but I thought I might as well master-mind it. "I could take a guess," I said. "A guy named Frankie Brand, maybe." I saw by their expressions I was right. "Has he confessed?"

"Not yet," Malikoff said dryly. "He was dead when we found him. With two .38 bullets in his heart, a few miscellaneous diamonds in his pocket—and a jade necklace belonging to Miss Linda Leyton wrapped tastefully around his neck."

That stopped me. I'd expected to light a slow fuse under the jewelry thieves, but I hadn't expected to get that kind of action for my money. It meant I was going to have to revise some of my ideas.

"Well?" Malikoff said patiently.

"Not so well," I admitted. "I did have an idea that Frankie Brand was in on these robberies, and I'll admit I thought they'd pick Miss Leyton last night, but that's about it."

"But not all?" Wayne asked.

"You can damn well bet it isn't all." Malikoff said. "I've worked with this joker too often. If he knew that much, you can bet he wasn't just sitting around, and you can bet even more that he has some idea what the next step is going to be."

"I had a better idea an hour ago than I do know," I said. I saw the way they were looking at me and threw up my hands.

"Look, boys, I'll admit I'm partly responsible for your getting Frankie, but this isn't what I was expecting to happen. Right this minute I can't lay it out any cleaner than you can. The best I can do is tell you why Frankie was killed."

"Why?"

"Where's Miss Layton's necklace?" I asked.

"We're still holding it as evidence. She'll get it back later."

"Don't bother," I said. "The one you found on Frankie is paste. That's probably why he was killed—although it's a pretty good bet he would have been killed anyway."

"Where's the real necklace?"

"I know where it is," I said, not bothering to answer that it was right in my pocket that moment. "It'll be back to her by tonight."

"You know," Lieutenant Wayne said, leaning back and looking up at the ceiling, "I've been working day and night, and I've been taking quite a riding from the Commissioner, the Inspector, the Captain, and even that Fancy Dan who works for the insurance company. All of this, you understand, without getting my hands on anything or anybody. I think maybe I'd like to question somebody. You feel like a little session, Murray?"

"Sure," agreed Malikoff, grinning. "I've been wanting to get this boy under a rubber hose ever since I first met him."

They were kidding, but not entirely. I knew exactly how they felt, but I also knew that I couldn't give them any more than I had.

"Look, boys," I said, "I'm not playing hard to get, but it's got to be played my way. Give me twelve hours. By that time, we'll either have it all sewed up—or you might as well throw me in the nearest cell."

"What do you think, Murray?" Wayne asked, without looking at me.

"It's worth it," Malikoff said. "The chance of really throwing him in the can is worth anything we have to go through."

"Okay, Milo," agreed Wayne. "You've got twelve hours. Exactly on the nose. If we haven't heard from you by then, we'll put out a pick-up call on you. Now, beat it before I change my mind."

I did.

Originally, my idea had been to get close to Frankie Brand after he'd copped the paste necklace, and then stick there. But there wasn't much point in getting close to a corpse. I'd had a glimmer of another idea, which I'd discarded, but now I fished it back out of my memory. It would have to do. I'd been fairly lucky so far; so maybe I could push it a little more.

I went downtown to the neighborhood where Whistles lived. I picked up a discarded piece of wrapping paper and on it I wrote myself a letter. Then I bought an envelope in a novelty store, rubbed it around in the gutter a little, and addressed it. I sent the letter by special delivery.

I checked upon Whistles and found he was still in the rooming house where I'd stashed him. Then I went over to a secondhand clothes shop and picked up the worst suit and hat I could find. I went back to my apartment.

When I got there, I called the office. Peaches-and-Cream answered.

"Honey, this is Milo," I said. "First, don't let anyone know I'm calling."

"But Mr. Bancroft will be angry," she said. "He's had me calling every bar in town for two days."

"That's why I don't want you to tell anyone I called. Look, there's going to be a special delivery letter for me pretty soon. When it comes, just put it in on my desk like a good girl and keep your mouth shut."

"But—" she began.

I put the receiver down gently. When the phone rang a few minutes later. I didn't bother to answer it.

I had one more call to make—to Linda. She was pretty cold at first, but I finally convinced her that I hadn't just called on her in my professional capacity and that I hadn't been hanging around to keep her from being robbed. The last was strictly true. After a while her voice softened and she agreed to see me again that night.

About five o'clock, I called the office again and asked Peaches-and-Cream about the special delivery letter. She said it had been delivered. Then she double-crossed me. I heard the connection being made and then Niels's voice.

"Milo," he bellowed, "where—"

I hung up on him. I waited a few minutes, then I called Lieutenant Malikoff. I told him what I had to say and hung up before he could give me any argument. The phone was ringing as I left the apartment. I grinned, wondering which one of them it was.

I went down to Whistles's former rooming house.

I let myself into the dingy little room and switched on the

single blue bulb. It seemed to smell even worse than it had before. I sat down on the edge of the bed and lit a cigarette. I couldn't decide which looked worse, the bedclothes or the suit I was wearing. It wasn't long before I began to itch. I was sure it was imagination, but that didn't make me itch any less.

It was a long, tiring wait. As night began to really get under way, I could hear the rooming house come to life. Listless footsteps moved around. Here and there I could hear hacking coughs. Once, in the room above me, someone started to fight, but they evidently didn't have the energy to keep it up long.

I'd been in the room about an hour when I heard the strident and complaining voice of the landlady as she led someone upstairs to the room across from the one I was in. I couldn't make out the words, but she kept complaining and a masculine voice kept answering. At last she gave up and went away. There was silence from the other room.

It must have been two hours later. The room was blue with smoke. I'd just got rid of a bad leg cramp and the itching was worse than ever. Then I heard footsteps coming softly up the stairs. They came along the hallway, scuffing gently along the worn carpet, and stopped in front of my door.

A trickle of sweat ran down my back beneath the shirt.

The knock was barely audible.

"Who's there?" I asked. I didn't have to work at it to make my voice sound like a crook's. It came naturally.

"Milo March," said the voice on the other side of the door.

I grinned crookedly and shifted on the bed. "Come in," I said.

The door opened and he came inside. And right then he

proved that I'd made another wrong guess. I'd figured he'd come in and try to find out something. But I was wrong. He wanted only one answer and he didn't have to ask any questions to get it.

The minute his eyes were adjusted to the dim blue light and he spotted me, he lifted the gun in his hand and started to squeeze the trigger.

I think it was something about the way he stood that tipped me off more than anything else. I threw myself sideways off the bed and prayed that I'd make it.

I did—just. In that small room, the gun sounded like a cannon, but I still heard the thud of the bullet hitting the bed. Then I was on the floor, rolling and clawing under the tattered coat for my own gun. I came to a stop on my belly, with the gun out.

He was bringing his gun down for another shot. I could see he was surprised, but not so much that it was slowing him up any. I didn't have any time for real fancy shooting, but I pointed in the general direction of his right kneecap and pulled the trigger.

I was right about one thing: a vice-president can scream just as loudly as anyone else.

He was still flopping around on the floor and yelling when the door across the hall opened and Blair Wayne and Murray Malikoff came charging in. They had their guns out, but they saw they wouldn't need them. And, as though his audience was complete, Hanley fainted. I wasn't too surprised; most people will faint sooner or later when they've got a smashed kneecap.

"Hanley!" Lieutenant Wayne said as he leaned over the figure on the floor. He sounded almost happy.

"Hanley," I said. I stood up and leaned on the dresser. My own knees were shaking slightly. It had been a little closer than I liked to have things work out.

"I thought you were going to get him to talk," Malikoff said.

"So did I," I said, "but he had other ideas. Don't worry. He'll talk when he comes to. He's just lost all his nerve."

"What's all this?" Wayne asked, waving at the room. "You going to a masquerade?"

"Just trying to look enough like Whistles Naylor to fool him," I said. "I guess it worked." I lit a cigarette. "He'll tell us where the jewels are. There should be about five and a half million's worth hidden somewhere—maybe even in his hotel room."

"I like it this way," Wayne said, nudging Hanley with the toe of his shoe. "This is going to make up for a lot of things that have been happening. But how did you get on to him, Milo?"

"It was mostly guesswork," I admitted. "When he and I were working together, he got on my nerves, just like he did on yours, mostly by yapping about finding a pattern in the crimes. There didn't seem to me to be any to find. But when I walked out and got away from him long enough to think, I realized there *was* one pattern. The robberies—that is, the choice of houses—seemed to be related to his plan of covering the policyholders in advance. And it suddenly occurred to me that he was also the answer to how someone was getting in and out of houses that were guarded.

"Blair, you complained about his practically running your department—well, the point was that he always knew the exact location of every cop, so it was easy for him to plan for someone else to get in and out of the house without being seen. And, in his role of insurance man, he'd been able to get a complete layout of the house and the location of the jewels. Not to mention that everyone would obligingly call him up and let him know when they wouldn't be home. Frankie Brand was the boy he'd hired to pull the jobs. Probably he hired a different guy in each city,"

"What about the fencing?"

"He didn't fence the jewels," I said. "He let Frankie think they were being fenced right away, and he was paying Frankie off in cash. But he'd held on to them. I suppose he planned to work a deal with the companies. He told me himself that the companies would be willing to pay a million dollars for all the jewelry back, and no questions asked."

Malikoff whistled. "I guess that explains why he was willing to take the chance. A million dollars is a lot of dough, even for a vice-president."

I nodded, "I thought it might be Hanley, but I knew it would be tough to prove it. I figured that Frankie was working with him. I got a copy of Miss Leyton's necklace made and then switched them. I knew, if it was Hanley, that he'd spot it as a phony right away and he'd jump to the conclusion that Frankie was double-crossing him. I thought that would start to crack it open, but I didn't think he'd kill Frankie. I guess I started out with so much contempt for a guy like Hanley, I never thought he had that kind of nerve."

"I know what you mean," Malikoff said.

"So then I had to switch my plans," I said. "I had planned on sticking close to Frankie and being around when a blowup came. With Frankie dead, I tried this: I sent myself a special delivery note today. It purported to come from Whistles Naylor. The note said if I'd come around tonight, he'd tell me where to find the jade necklace, and he'd tell me who Frankie had been working for. I told the girl to leave the letter on my desk.

"I knew Hanley would look at it. It would be easy for him to find out from Niels that I often get information from Whistles. It would also be easy for him to find Whistles's address in my files. And no matter how careful he'd been, he couldn't be positive that somebody like Whistles hadn't seen him one of the times he contacted Frankie. If he was guilty, he'd have to come down to shut up Whistles. Only I was there instead."

"Sounds good," Malikoff said. "This is probably the gun he used on Frankie, and that'll make it easier."

"Now all you have to do is get him to talk about the jewels," I said.

"He'll talk," Wayne said grimly. "What about Miss Leyton's real necklace?"

"I've got it right here," I said. I took out the box and showed it to him. "I'm taking it back to her now. As soon as I can go home and change clothes, I have a date with Miss Leyton to listen to some more jazz."

"Jazz?" Wayne said, with interest. "I didn't know you went in for that. What kind?"

"Strictly Dixie," I said. "I figure on starting out tonight with

Louis Armstrong's 'West End Blues,' the Memphis Five's 'Rampart Street Blues,' Barney Bigard's 'Minuet Blues,' and maybe Bix Beiderbecke's 'Jazz Me Blues.' "

"I go for those blues myself," Wayne said dreamily. "I guess maybe my favorite is Bessie Smith singing the 'Empty Bed Blues.' You got that one?"

"I got it," I said. I grinned at him. "But I don't think we're going to play that one tonight. ... Take good care of that ice when you find it, boys. Don't forget, I worked hard to get it back."

4

Murder for Madame

It was one of those days when everything seemed to be slightly out of focus. I'd been out on the town the night before and had a few rations of brandy, but that wasn't it. It was one of those times you wake up and right away you know it's a day when all the favorites are going to fall on their faces. I went to the office and waited for something to happen.

The office is the Inter-World Insurance Service Corporation in the Gilmore Building in Denver, on the tenth floor. Presided over by a receptionist with peaches-and-cream skin and blue-black hair, with the kind of figure that would make a convalescent leap out of his wheelchair and start climbing walls. But it would be a wasted climb. This girl had "I do" in her eyes; she was going to play strictly for keeps or she wasn't going to play. I knew, because I'd tried.

I managed to kill half the day just sitting in my office. There was a bottle of brandy in my desk drawer and I'd used up a couple of inches of it when my phone rang. It was Peaches-and-Cream.

"You can wake up, Milo," she said. "I guess there's a case for you."

"A case?" I said. "I can't even finish a bottle without somebody interrupting me, so what will I do with a case?"

"Very funny. But he wants to see you." She switched off.

I finished the brandy in my glass, lit a cigarette, and stood up. Milo March, chief and only investigator for Inter-World, was about to go to work.

He was Niels Bancroft, owner and president of Inter-World. His office was right next to mine, but that was the only thing they had in common. Mine had a simple frosted glass door with *Milo March* in small black letters; his was solid oak, about as simple as a vault door at Fort Knox.

I walked out of my office, stopped to admire the receptionist for a minute, then opened the door and stepped inside.

Niels Bancroft is a big man, looking a little like an ex-pug. His hair is gray and there are gray tufts thrusting from his ears. He's a chain smoker—sticks half the cigarette in his mouth. He lights cigarettes with old-fashioned kitchen matches, but he wears $200 suits and a $500 watch.

He looked up as I entered and motioned me to a chair.

"How's it going, Milo?" he asked. His tone indicated that he didn't really care how it was going.

"It's one of those days," I said. "If something screwy doesn't happen, I'm going to lose my faith in intuition."

He looked at me queerly. "It's happened," he said flatly.

I felt better. "What's the case?"

"It really isn't a case," he said. "But I promised we'd look into it when she kept insisting. If it's screwiness you want, this is it."

I asked questions with my eyebrows.

"Mrs. George B. Denning," he said. "She carries about a hundred and fifty thousand dollars of jewelry insurance. With Great Northern, including the coverage on a five-thousand-dollar pearl necklace she bought in Paris three weeks ago. Last night someone broke into the house and stole the box the pearls came in."

"What about the pearls?"

"Dumped them out on the dressing table and left them."

"Too heavy?" I asked.

He glared at me. "Don't be funny. Maybe the guy just likes boxes."

"What does the dame expect us to do?"

"I explained to her that the insurance doesn't cover the box the pearls came in," Niels said, "but she wasn't listening much. She told me that the box had sentimental value, then suggested that whoever took the box might come back for the pearls. I said I'd send you out to talk to her."

I looked him over. I'd known Niels Bancroft a long time. I liked him. But he was a guy who wouldn't give anyone the right time unless they first gave him a watch.

"You can't bill Great Northern for this," I said slowly, "so what's the catch?"

He looked like he was going to be evasive, but he changed his mind. "Mrs. Denning said something very interesting," he said. "She told me the box had sentimental value because if it hadn't been for it she wouldn't have met Henri. Mrs. Denning's husband's first name is George. Mr. Denning is about sixty-five. Mrs. Denning is a young chick. Get it?"

"I've heard of such things," I said dryly. "But where do we

come in? We're an insurance company, remember, not some private eye outfit who can give the old man a bill for slipping him the bad news."

"Wives with a yen," he grunted, "aren't good insurance risks. There's a morals clause in her policy. Great Northern might like to know it if she's playing around with some young guy who just might elope with the family jewels some night. We'll be looking after the client's affairs—we can probably bill them for a supplementary report."

"So that's it," I said. "I'm to talk like I'm looking for the box, but keep an eye out for any hanky-panky. Eye to the keyhole and all that sort of stuff. It's a wonder you don't suggest I lead her astray myself just so you can charge for a report."

"You need suggestions?" he said. He grinned at me. "Get to work, Milo. Here's the file on the case. Look it over."

"Wrap it up," I told him. I picked up the file and went back to my own office.

There wasn't much in the file. I'd made the original report and there had been nothing at the time to indicate that the wife wasn't in love with her husband despite the forty years' difference in age. But that had been five years earlier, and maybe her interests had broadened. I made a note of the address and started out.

"Don't tell me you're finally going to work," the reception-ist said. "I thought they had retired you."

"Just saving me for the big game," I said. "Just like in the movies, I'm going out to look into the matter of a burglar who doesn't like pearls and a babe who maybe doesn't like her husband."

"Milo March, the answer to dissatisfied wives," she said, laughing. "That's about your speed."

"People who always stay in low gear shouldn't talk about speed," I told her, and left before she could think up an answer.

The Dennings lived in the gold coast section of Denver. One of those twenty-room shacks where even the servants have servants. I wondered if the neighbors ran back and forth borrowing cups of diamonds.

A butler answered the door. He was putting a price tag on my suit with his eyes while I was telling him who I was and who I wanted to see. I think he toyed with the idea of telling me to go around to the back door, but he finally let me step into the foyer. Then he went off to get a ruling on my presence.

When he came back, he'd resigned himself to the inevitable. He led me up to the second floor and into a small study. Its walls were lined with books, most of them Book of the Month Club choices, looking unread.

There were two people already in the study. One of them was a young man, just a shade too handsome. He had wavy black hair, soft black eyes, and a lot of white teeth. When I entered, he rippled to his feet and for a moment I thought he was either going to click his heels or curtsy.

The other one was a dish. Her blond hair, poodle cut, made a halo of curls around her head. She wore some kind of black robe that just missed being sheer. It clung to her body in a way that offered proof that her curves and hollows were really her own. After seeing her in that robe, anyone who still had to use his imagination was in a bad way.

When I got around to looking at her face, I discovered she was looking me over in the same fashion. There was a challenge in her eyes as her gaze met mine.

"Mr. March?" she asked. Her voice was like a built-in caress. I nodded.

"I'm Arlene Denning," she said. "This is Henri, Mr. March. Henri Ormont."

The pretty boy had been watching us, and he hadn't liked the way we'd looked each other over. There was a touch of hardness in his voice when he spoke. "M'sieu March," he said. He gave me his hand as though it was something he didn't want any longer. I shook it and gave it back to him.

"An old friend of the family?" I asked her, playing it straight.

"Henri?" She laughed, "I should say not. He's my protégé."

"Oh?" I said, giving it just enough inflection. I looked the pretty boy over again. "What does he do? Recite?"

His face got darker and he opened his mouth. He was going to say something but her laughter cut him short. She was playing around with him, all right, but it hadn't spoiled her sense of humor.

"Henri is a singer," she said. "He has the most divine voice, and I'm going to sponsor him here. Would you care to hear him sing, Mr. March?"

"I can hardly wait," I said dryly, "but I'll keep a stiff upper lip and manage somehow. I'd rather hear him sing about the robbery last night."

He got a frown on his forehead. *"Pardon?"* he said.

" 'To sing,' " she said, "is American slang meaning to talk or to tell. Mr. March may mean that he thinks you have something important to tell about the robbery." She suddenly decided not to be amused anymore.

"If that's the case, I'm afraid Mr. March is overstepping his authority."

"Sure," I said easily. I sat down and looked at them. "You want to talk about me or about the box that was stolen?"

"This man is insulting," Henri said. He had only a slight accent. "Why not phone the company and report him, *chérie?"*

"There's the phone," I said before she could answer. I lit a cigarette. "But I'm afraid you'll have to put up with my bad manners if you want us to even listen. We haven't insured any boxes."

It was easy to read both of them. She was partly angry and partly amused, but he didn't see anything to be amused about. If she'd given him the nod, he would have tried to take a punch at me.

"It is rather peculiar," she said finally, "but I would appreciate it, Mr. March, if you will try to find the missing box. If you succeed, I will be very grateful." Her eyes added that I'd like the way she showed her gratitude.

"Tell me about it," I said.

"There isn't much to tell, Mr. March. The pearls were in the box on the dresser in my room. My husband was on a business trip yesterday and was not going to be home until late, so Henri and I had dinner at a small club. The Blue Pheasant. We danced for a while after dinner, then came back here. We were in this room, playing records until about midnight. Then … I went to my room and discovered that somebody had stolen the box containing the pearls, although the pearls were on the dressing table. The lock on the French window was broken. I—we believe it had been pried open with some sort of tool."

"You called the police?"

"No. We—well, to be truthful, we were afraid they'd only laugh at us since the only article stolen had no actual value."

"What kind of a box was it?"

"About this big," she said. She showed me with her hands. It must have been about five inches long, maybe three inches wide, and almost two and a half inches deep. "I believe it was made of some sort of wood, then was covered with leather on the outside. The inside is lined with black velvet."

"Why do you think it was stolen?" I asked. "Why do you think anyone would toss out a five-thousand-dollar-necklace and take a worthless box?"

"I don't know, Mr. March," she said. I had the feeling she was telling the truth.

"One reads in the papers," Henri said, "that in America there are criminals who are—how do you say it?—psychotic."

"We've got our share of nuts," I said, "but I never heard of any so cracked he'd throw away five grand. Tell me something else—if this box is so worthless, why do you want it back?"

They looked at each other. "It has sentimental value," she said. "It would mean nothing to others, but to Henri and me it means very much. We'd give a lot to have it back."

"You understand," Henri said, "we do not want to have the man arrested. We thought perhaps you could find the person who took it and tell us. We could then, perhaps, buy it back from him. You understand?"

I didn't, but I nodded. This case was more than screwy. There was something wrong about the whole setup. If there were a burglar crazy enough to throw away a pearl necklace and take a worthless box, then he might be crazy enough to refuse any offer to buy it back.

"How did it get all this sentimental value?" I asked.

"I bought the pearl necklace," she said, "in a little shop on the rue de Chalmonte in Paris. I had just bought it when Henri came along and stopped to admire the box. That was the way we met."

"He didn't admire the pearls?" I asked dryly.

"The pearls are nice," Henri admitted, "but I have seen many fine pearls. I admired the box, M'sieur, because one seldom sees jewelry boxes today which are handmade. This one was."

"It's not what you think, Mr. March," she said and managed to be a little annoyed. "Just before Henri stopped, there was another man who came to the counter and tried to get acquainted with me. He was interested in the pearls." She laughed. "He tried to buy them from me. When that failed, he then thought of trying to take me to dinner."

"Oh, well," I said, "some men prefer pearls and some prefer jewel boxes. Can I see the jimmied window?"

The dish nodded and told me to follow her. I didn't mind at all; it was a nice view from there. The only one who didn't enjoy it was Henri, who went along and watched me.

The lock had been pried open, all right. From the outside. I could see the marks in the wood. In fact, there were so many of them, it looked to me like an amateur job. Now, if it had been the pearls that were missing, I would have nominated Henri. But it hadn't been the pearls, and Henri seemed to want the box back as much as she did, maybe more.

I told them I'd see what I could do and left them in the bedroom. They were staring into each other's eyes. Maybe she was going to give him a singing lesson.

I'd just started down the long hallway when the butler appeared, popping out of a doorway as though he'd been lying in ambush. "This way, sir," he said. He took off in a direction that definitely didn't lead to the front door, but I followed.

He finally stopped in front of a door, opened it, and ushered me into another study. "This is Mr. March, sir," he said, and left.

The man who sat behind the desk was about sixty-five and looked it, in a dignified sort of way. His hair was white and so was his clipped mustache. He was a Man of Distinction, with or without a glass in his hand.* But there was a look of pain in his blue eyes that indicated his life wasn't all roses and dividends.

I could guess who he was, but I didn't say anything. He'd brought me here. It was his move.

"Mr. March," he said, "you are from the insurance company?"

"In a way," I said. "I'm from the Inter-World Insurance Service Corporation. We represent the company which holds your jewelry policy."

"Do you have identification?" he wanted to know.

I nodded and got out my wallet. I opened it to the proper card and shoved it over to him. He glanced at it and handed it hack.

"Sorry for seeming to doubt you, Mr. March," he said. "It's just that I like to be sure. I'm George B. Denning."

I nodded again and waited. It was his ball.

"You've talked with Mrs. Denning about the—ah—robbery of last evening?"

I admitted that I had.

"I'm aware," he said, "that our insurance does not cover the

---

* A reference to magazine ads for Lord Calvert Canadian whiskey, "for Men of Distinction."

theft of a box. Mrs. Denning, however, seems attached to that box for some reason or other. I'd appreciate anything you can do. Your company may bill me for any charges."

For some reason, maybe it was the expression in his eyes, I felt sorry for him. He must have known his wife was a tramp, but he was still going to try to give her everything she wanted. That probably included Henri.

"We don't work that way," I said. I decided to stretch a point. "But there's always the chance that whoever took the box may come back later for the jewelry. So I'll look into it."

"Thank you," he said. "Roberts will show you out."

Roberts popped up as soon as I left the study. I tried to pump him a little as we went toward the door, but it was like trying to find water in Death Valley. He had one answer for everything. "I couldn't say, sir." He was a great conversationalist.

"Well," I said when we reached the door, "it's been nice chatting with you, Roberts. We must try it again sometime when you're alive." I closed the door and went back into the world.

There was no reason why we should do anything about this case, but I was curious. It was screwy enough that anyone would steal the thing in the first place; the fact that the owner wanted it back so badly was just too much. I was going to look into it.

I drove down to a different section Denver. If the Dennings live in the gold coast, this was tin can alley. There was a little junkie living down there who was the Louella Parsons* of

---

* The legendary Hollywood gossip columnist.

the underworld. He knew almost everything that was going on, and for a price—usually enough for a couple of needles of heroin—he'd publish a private edition.

His name was Whistles Naylor. Once it had probably been something-else Naylor, but the name had long been lost. He was known as Whistles because of the habit of blowing the whistle on others. The only reason he was still living was that the few times his story had been really important, the leading character hadn't been around afterwards.

Whistles Naylor lived in one small room in a broken-down rooming house. I knew he'd probably be in. He never showed in daylight unless it was to get a fix.

I went up the broken stairs and knocked on his door. There was a rustling sound inside as though there were mice, then silence.

"Who's there?" he finally asked, his voice barely reaching through the door.

"Milo March," I said.

There was another wait while he was making sure that he remembered my voice. Then the door opened just enough for me to slip in.

The room looked a mess and smelled worse. The fact that the only light came from a small blue bulb didn't help the sight any, although Whistles would have looked just as bad under any light. He was a little guy, with a face as much like a rat's as it could get and still be human. His face was twitching and I knew he hadn't had a shot for several hours.

"Didn't know whether to let you in," he said. He shuffled across the room and sat on the dirty bed, looking at me out of the corners of his eyes. "I thought maybe it was the old dame with one of her tricks. She's been looking for the rent scratch."

I lit a cigarette. It helped to offset the smell of dirt and cooked heroin. Some, but not much. "I need something, Whistles," I said. "Maybe you can help me out."

"Gee, Milo, I don't know," he said. He sniffed loudly. "Things have been pretty quiet. I ain't heard of no big jobs in flashy stuff."

"I'm not looking for any thing big," I told him. "You heard anything about a guy who lifted a box last night?"

He looked at me like he thought I'd blown a fuse. "You joy popping, Milo?" he asked.

"Not even a skin pop," I said, grinning. "This guy broke into a house and took a jewelry box, after carefully dumping out a pearl necklace and leaving it. He jimmied the window, so he must have wanted the box bad. He might have been an amateur."

He started to shake his head, then stopped in the middle of it and looked surprised. "Maybe," he said. "You know Lew Pisano, Milo?"

The name sounded familiar, but I couldn't place it.

"A second-story man," he added.

Then I remembered him. I'd come across him a couple of times. A tough customer. He'd always been after big stuff and been pretty successful. He'd been sent away once, but that was all. And he wasn't the type to leave pearls lying around.

I shook my head. "I've always heard Pisano was a smooth worker. This guy left jimmy marks all over the place."

"Wait a minute," he said eagerly. "I'm just remembering something I heard last night. I'm in Three Fingers's joint and I hear Lew talking to a couple of other guys. He was telling him how some guy hired him to pull a job. He didn't say what the job was, but I heard him say the guy gave him a grand to grab something that wasn't worth more than a couple of bucks and he thought the guy was nuts. That could've maybe been the box."

"Could be," I said. "Go ahead."

"Lew didn't pull the job," he said. "He went out to pull it last night, but somebody had beat him to it. He's trying to find out who."

It was beginning to get complicated. Now there were three guys who wanted that empty jewelry box. The guy who'd hired Lew Pisano, the guy who got the box, and Henri. Four, if you counted me, and I was beginning to want a look at it myself. I wondered if Henri had maybe used the box to smuggle something into the country.

"Where does Lew hang out?" I asked Whistles.

"He lives in the Daly Hotel. Later at night you can usually find him at Three Fingers." Whistles was watching me and trying to control the shaking of his hands. He knew that I always come across with something, and he was in a bad way.

I gave him twenty bucks and got out of there. On the way, I stopped and covered his rent with the sloppy old dame who ran the rooming house.

The Daly Hotel was owned by one of our leading criminals, and a lot of the boys lived there. I stopped off at a drugstore a half block away and phoned Lew Pisano. He was still in his room. When he answered, I hung up.

I parked the car where I could watch the front of the hotel, and when Lew came out I talked to him. He was the best bet I had. He could at least lead me to the man who'd hired him, and that might even eventually lead me to the guy we were both looking for. If not, I still might get a hint about why that box was so popular.

For four hours I tailed Pisano without getting anywhere. He stopped in at a horse room, went and had a few drinks with some characters who were better know at police headquarters than anywhere else, and then spent a couple of hours in the apartment of a flashy blonde while I sat across the street in my car. It was beginning to look like a bust, but he was still the only lead I had, so I stuck to him.

When he finally left the apartment, he went straight to a little nightclub downtown. It was one of those places where they always kept the lights at half mast, so I gave him enough time to get settled and then followed him in.

I stopped at the bar and had a brandy. While I was drinking it, I looked the place over. A bored trio—piano, bass fiddle, and drums—was beating the hell out of some music that deserved better treatment. It was "West End Blues," although anyone who'd ever heard Louis Armstrong play it might have had trouble recognizing it. The club was only about one-fourth full. There were booths along two walls, and I finally spotted Lew Pisano sitting alone in one of those. A waiter was bringing him something to eat, so it looked like we'd be there for a while.

I paid my bar check and went to one of the booths on the other side of the room where I could keep an eye on Lew. I ordered another brandy and some food. It was past my dinner hour and I was hungry.

Maybe thirty minutes later Lew got company. I'd never seen him before. He looked more like a successful businessman than Lew's usual friends, so I guessed he was the one who hired him for the job. He looked pretty sore.

Then I got my first surprise. Someone else came in and joined them. A handsome, well-dressed young man with a pretty smile. Henri. He and the second man both knew each other.

A moment later I got my second surprise. Someone else came along my side of the club. She was wearing a hooded cape and was being careful not to be seen by anyone on the other side of the room. She was about to enter the booth next to mind when I recognized her.

"Mrs. Denning," I called, just loud enough for her to hear.

She was startled and, for a moment I think, frightened. Then she recognized me. She came over and slipped into the seat across from me.

"Hello," she said. She was still shaken, but she was recovering fast. "I—I just felt like going somewhere by myself and dropped in here. I wasn't expecting to see you, Mr. March."

I'm sure you weren't," I said. "Do you make a habit of trailing Henri whenever he leaves you?"

She thought about it a minute and then decided that there was no point to pretending. "I did follow him," she said. "Something strange happened after you left today. Henri received a telephone call and wouldn't tell me anything about it. So when he insisted on coming out alone tonight, I followed him."

"To see if he was meeting another woman?"

"Maybe," she said. There was a lot of wisdom in her smile. The wrong kind of wisdom. "I'll confess that was my first thought. But I see I was wrong. Who are those men he's with?"

"I don't know one of them," I told her, "but the other is one of Denver's leading citizens. He's quite often in some of our better homes, but usually late at night, and never by invitation. He has a liking for other people's jewelry."

"You mean he's the one—"

I shook my head. "He was supposed to get the box, but someone beat him to it. That's probably the most popular empty box in the city, Mrs. Denning."

"The name's Arlene," she said. She'd gotten over her initial surprise and now she had another look in her eyes. "Why does everyone want that jewel box, Milo?"

"You don't know?" I asked her, and she shook her head.

"I've only had one idea," I said slowly. I lit two cigarettes and handed her one. "It sounds to me like the box was pretty thick. Maybe thick enough to have a false bottom. And there might have been something that Henri—and his friends there—wanted to get into America without paying duty. That would explain Henri's sentimental attachment to it."

She didn't care too much for that. "You think so?" she asked coolly. "You don't think a man might be sentimental about an object because he met me through it?"

"Not a grown man," I said. "That belongs to adolescence.

Now, a man might become sentimental about you, he might even become lustful—but not about a box."

I was watching the three men in the booth. The older, well-dressed man was talking with a great deal of controlled emphasis.

"Milo," she said.

I looked at her. She was leaning forward and per plunging neckline was plunging even more. The view would have stirred a wooden Indian. She knew it, too. She saw the direction of my gaze and laughed softly. Her eyes were bright.

"To hell with Henri," she said. "I did follow him here because I thought he might be meeting with another woman. Now I don't care if he does. We could have fun together, Milo."

I was watching the three men again. The older one had taken something from his pocket that looked like a telegram. He showed it to the other two. Lew Pisano had a paper and pencil and was copying something from it.

"Sure, honey," I said. "We could make beautiful music together."

The telegram, if that's what it was, went back into the older man's pocket and he stood up. He said something else to Lew and Henri, and turned away from the booth.

"Then why don't we?" she asked. She sounded breathless.

I watched the older man near the front of the club. Then I turned back to her and that plunging neckline.

"There's one reason, honey," I said. "Somebody's playing a sour note offstage. I think I'd better go do some tuning up. You keep a light burning in the window for me."

I stood up and tossed a bill on the table. I leaned over and planted a fast kiss on her blond hair and then I left before she could think of an answer.

The man was just getting into a taxi in front of the club. My car was parked a half block up ahead. I hurried to it and pulled away from the curb in time to follow the cab.

A few minutes later, the taxi pulled up in front of one of our better hotels. The Georgian House. There was only one parking place near the hotel. We entered the elevator together. There were several other people in the elevator, so the operator didn't even notice that I failed to ask for a floor. My man asked for the fourth.

We both got out on the fourth floor. He turned to the right, so I turned to the left. I stopped in front of the first door I came to and watched him out of the corner of my eye. He paid no attention to me.

When he'd gone into his room, I walked down and stood in front of it. I had two choices. I could go downstairs and find out who was registered for this room. But all that would give me was a name. It wouldn't tell me anything about why he wanted an empty jewel box badly enough to pay a thousand dollars for it. And I wanted a look at that telegram.

There was no point doing everything the safe way. I slipped the gun from my holster and held it just inside my coat. Then I knocked on the door.

He opened the door and looked at me. *"Chto vy khoti—"* he started to say. Then he looked annoyed and switched to English. "What do you want?" he asked. He had a fairly heavy accent. That made it sound even more like some kind of smuggling game.

"I want to talk to you," I said. I still kept the gun out of sight. "About an empty jewelry box."

That got him. A shrewd look came into his face. "Come in," he said. He held the door open and I went in. I took a quick look around. He had two rooms, but the door was open to the second one and there was no one else in sight. I turned to face him.

"You have it?" he asked. "How much?"

I shook my head. "I don't have it." I moved my hand and let him see the gun. "I want to know about it."

I had to say one thing for him. Guns didn't scare him. His face clouded with anger. "Who are you?" He demanded.

"Just a guy who's interested in boxes," I said.

He said something in his own language. It didn't sound like a compliment. "Get out," he added in English.

"When you've told me why everybody wants that box," I told him. I waved the gun to emphasize it, but he didn't pay any attention: I doubt if he ever saw it.

"Then I will call the police," he said. He started to walk to the phone. I couldn't know whether he was bluffing or intended to really call the police, or was hoping to trick me in some way. But I'd gone too far to change my mind and start walking back now.

I took a deep breath and hoped I wasn't making a mistake. Then I put the barrel of my gun against the side of his head. There was a satisfying *thwunk* and he dropped to the floor. I put the gun away and knelt beside him. I did a thorough frisk job on him.

A few minutes later, I had the telegram and his other papers in my hand, and they felt like they weighed a ton. I'd followed him into his room expecting to pick a plum of information; instead I'd hit the jackpot and I wasn't sure that I liked it even a little bit.

The telegram was from the Russian Embassy in Washington. It was addressed to Dimitri Monevsky, who was apparently the guy on the floor, and it said there was an NTS man, named Alexis Dubinov, in Denver, and it gave the address where he could be found. The rest of the papers identified Dimitri Monevsky as a Soviet representative in America with full diplomatic privileges and immunity.

I had slugged my way into the middle of a first-class international incident—unless I could find something to pin on him. I copied the address in the telegram and stuffed the papers back in his pockets. Then I did a pretty quick job of going over his two rooms.

When I'd finished, I still didn't have any idea why a Soviet agent wanted an empty box. Even if I was right and the box wasn't empty, I couldn't see what a Soviet agent was doing in the picture. It certainly had me puzzled.

I didn't want to be around when Comrade Monevsky came to, so I beat it out of there. I had an idea that the next scene was going to be played at the address that had been in the telegram, and if I hurried I might still get there to catch Lew Pisano in his opening. Maybe I could even play a walk-on bit myself.

My car was still parked in front of the hydrant and there wasn't a ticket on it. I got in and drove off.

The address was over in an older, cheaper part of town. When I got there, it turned out to be an old four-story brick building, with outside fire escapes, that had been turned into low rental apartments.

I went in and took a quick look at the mailboxes. Dubinov was top floor rear. As I turned to leave, someone brushed past me and went in with his key. I was tempted to follow him so I could get inside without ringing anyone's bell, but I didn't do it. I could always get in later.

I went around the side of the building and looked up. The top rear was all dark. The pigeon wasn't at home. I was about to go back to my car and park for a stakeout when suddenly the lights went on. That must have been Dubinov who'd passed me in the hallway.

Then I had a bright idea. The outside fire escape was made to order—if I didn't get caught on it. I swung myself up to the bottom step and started climbing.

I was right. It was a good spot. Dubinov had his blinds down, but there was about three inches at the bottom. By crouching down on the fire escape, I could see fine.

The man in the room was short and chunky. He must have been about fifty, with a broad Slavic face. He'd taken off his coat and was sitting at a table. In front of him was the box—anyway, it was a jewel box that answered the description Arlene Denning had given me, and I assume it was the same. There wasn't much chance there were two of them.

He'd been working on the box with a long-bladed knife and he'd had some luck. Even from where I was I could see the lifted false bottom. Then right next to the box I saw something that took my breath away. Two pear-shaped diamonds, which looked perfectly matched and must have been fifty carats each. Real pigeon eggs. And the light off them was enough to blind a man. They were the real thing. I'd seen too many of them to doubt it. If they'd been in that false bottom, and that's the way it looked, no wonder everyone had wanted that box. Those two diamonds made Arlene Denning's necklace look like something out of Woolworth's.

Inside the room, the man was idly poking one of the diamonds with his finger, but he was staring at the box. Finally, he reached inside and ripped out the false bottom. Maybe he was expecting to find more diamonds. Then he did something that made me think maybe he was off his rocker.

The false bottom was made of paper-thin layers of plywood glued together. He man picked up the knife and began to methodically strip off the layers of wood, tossing each one on the table.

Suddenly he stopped. I heard it, too. Someone was knocking at the door to his apartment.

He called out something, but his voice was too muffled for me to hear what he said. There was an answering murmur from the direction of the door. Whatever was said must have satisfied him. He hesitated a minute, then went to open the door.

A moment later, he was stumbling back into the center of the room, starting to raise his hands. But he never made it. There was a shot and he crumpled to the floor. Lew Pisano came into my view. He was still holding the gun in his hand. He looked around the room, spotted the table, and headed for it.

I decided it was time for my bit. I swung my gun and the window shattered. At the same moment, I hugged the brick wall beside the window. There was another shot from inside the room and something took a chunk out of the blind. But there was just that one shot. Lew Pisano wasn't any mental giant, but he was bright enough to know that he'd be a clay pigeon inside that lighted room. I heard his quick steps and then the door slammed.

I reached through, unfastened the window, and then threw it up. Then I went inside. I could hear Lew running down the stairs.

The man on the floor was dead. I checked that first, but it was too late to do anything for him. I turned back to the table and got another surprise. The box was gone, but the two diamonds were still there in plain sight.

Two perfectly matched diamonds of fifty carats each are worth a pretty large package of the long green. On the other hand, Lew Pisano was a guy who normally wouldn't pass up a nickel in his grandmother's purse. Now he ignored two diamonds to make off with an empty box. It added up to two things. It showed how much Comrade Monevsky wanted that box and, considering the rate of pay, it indicated that maybe Lew Pisano was a little afraid of the Russian. If he hadn't been, he would have grabbed the diamonds and left the box regardless of how much it was wanted.

This time, I'd seen the box. I'd seen the false bottom torn out of it; parts of it were still scattered on the table. I knew the box was empty, so its popularity was even more interesting. And Lew Pisano was on his way, probably to deliver it to the Russian.

I scooped up the diamonds, dropped them into my pocket, and got out of there.

A car was disappearing around the nearest corner when I hit the street. That was probably Lew. I got in my own car and got it moving. He was close enough so that I might have caught up and tailed him to wherever he was going, but that would be drawing it a little too fine at the other end. So I took a chance that he was heading for the hotel. I took a shorter way, taking the wrong direction on a couple of one-way streets, and pushing the old crate for all she was worth.

When I reached the hotel, I double-parked in a spot where I could cover two streets and waited, with the motor running.

His car came down the side street from where I'd expected it and I had no trouble recognizing him. I breathed a sigh of relief when I saw he was alone. I'd expected Henri to be with him. I didn't have any plan; I'd have to play this one by ear.

There were no parking spaces in front of the hotel. Lew turned left and then pulled into the hotel parking lot. I pulled in behind him. The attendant gave him a ticket, then came back and gave me one. I gunned my car down toward the other end of the lot where Lew was already parking his car.

The lot was pretty well filled, but luckily there was an empty space just two cars away from where he was parking. Without trying to be artistic about it, I shot into the space, taking a few ounces of paint off one of the other cars. I shut off the motor while I was braking and had the door open as my car stopped. I heard the door on Lew's car slam shut. It was going to be close, but I could still catch him before he got out in the driveway where the attendant could see us.

I ran around the two other cars, pulling the gun form my holster.

"Hey, you," I called, just loud enough for him to hear me. "What the hell was the idea of bumping into my car back there?"

He'd started to walk toward the hotel, but he wheeled around at the sound of my voice. The light was way up in the center of the parking lot and his face was a dark shadow. "You're nuts," he said. "I didn't bump any car."

"You bumped my car," I said and kept on going. I was covering my gun with my hand so the light wouldn't glint on it. "One of those hit-and-run guys, huh?"

"Look, jerk—" he started to say. By this time I was in close and he must have caught a glimpse of my gun, because he suddenly stopped talking and went for his own gun.

I hit him on the jaw with the barrel of the gun and he folded like an accordion. I'd intended to do that anyway, so it didn't make any difference whether he'd gone for his gun or not.

I went through his pockets and found the box. Then I went back to my car, started the motor, and backed out. I had a quarter ready and handed it and the ticket to the guy at the gate. He looked surprised. "Changed my mind," I told him. "I'm used to a better-class lot."

He looked even more startled, but I drove away before he had a chance to decide I was crazy.

There was one thing I wanted to find out. I looked at my watch and thought maybe I could still catch a guy I knew. A few blocks from the hotel, I stopped and went into an office building. I went up to the fifth floor and saw I was in luck.

There was still a light in the office. It was the local office of the Federal Bureau of Investigation. I'd met the guy in charge—a collegiate-looking fellow named Merrick—a couple of times and once I'd done him a small favor.

The door was locked, but I rapped on it and in a minute Merrick opened it. He recognized me.

"Hello, March," he said. "What do you want?"

"Want to ask you something." I said. "I thought maybe I'd find you working late. Trying to pile up some overtime pay, is that it?"

He laughed and opened the door wider. I followed him inside to his desk. It was piled high with papers. I noticed that the top sheets had been turned over so nobody could take a fast look.

"Catching up on my paperwork," he said, gesturing toward the desk. "What can I do for you, March?"

"Ever hear of the NTS?" I asked. The look in his eyes sharpened, so I knew I'd come to the right place.

"Maybe," he said. What else do you know about it?"

"Suppose a guy belonged to it and the guy was a Russian?"

He nodded. "That's the NTS I know about," he said. "It's the Russian underground.* Why do you ask?"

"Russian underground?" I said. "I thought everybody in Russia loved Stalin."

"There's been a Russian underground for twenty years," he said. "Nobody knows how big it is—I doubt if they know themselves. As you might guess, it isn't a very poplar movement, and I understand a member seldom knows more than

---

* Narodno Trudovoi Soyuz, the National Alliance of Russian Solidarists.

any other member. They've done some pretty valuable work both inside Russia and from the outside. None of them, even the ones who are never inside the country, are very good insurance risks. So why are you asking about it, March?"

"Crossword puzzle," I said. I moved towards the door, waving my hand. "Thanks, Merrick. I'll just run along and fill in the puzzle now."

I didn't like the way he was looking at me, but I kept on going and he didn't say anything to stop me. As I closed the door, he was still staring at me with that expression that seemed to be guessing what size electric chair I'd take.

Downstairs, I got into my car and slumped down in the seat. I'd been a busy little bee for several hours and it was high time I started checking over my inventory. For a guy who'd just started out being curious about an empty box, I'd piled up quite a number of things.

So Alexis Dubinov, the man Lew Pisano had killed, had been a member of the Russian underground. That's what it had said in the telegram I'd found of Dimitri Monevsky. And that meant that Monevsky must be more than just a harm-less Embassy employee. And Henri was a little more than the smuggling gigolo I'd been thinking he was. Obviously, I had stumbled into something. It was equally obvious that I had no business there; despite the two big diamonds, there wasn't a thing that involved Inter-World or any of its clients. This was the time when a smart guy would have turned the whole thing over to the FBI and the Homicide Squad of the Denver police, and been done with it.

But nobody had ever made the mistake of calling me a smart

guy. I'd never been able to figure out all the clever deductions you see gumshoes doing in the movies and on TV. The only way I solved cases was by keeping everybody a little off balance and then sticking my neck way out.

The more I thought about it, the more I was determined to stick around. My testimony alone wouldn't be enough to convict Lew Pisano, and he'd be sure to have a good alibi. Even if they broke that down, there might be a good chance that Henri and Comrade Monevsky might come out with nothing worse than being shipped back home. Although I didn't admit it to myself, another important factor was that I might never find out the secret of the empty box if I washed my hands of the case and turned it over to the FBI.

After a while I had an idea that I liked. I got out of the car and found a drugstore that had phone booths. I went into a booth, dropped in my nickel, and dialed police headquarters.

"Homicide," I told the desk sergeant when he answered.

A moment later, another voice came on. "Homicide, Burns speaking," he said. That was Sergeant Burns, Lieutenant Murray Malikoff's partner. I knew him well, but I didn't bother identifying myself.

I gave him the address of the apartment and told him that he'd find a dead man on the top floor in the rear. A guy named Dubinov, I added.

"Who's this speaking?" the Sergeant asked.

I grinned and hung up. Then I went out to the car and drove straight home to my own apartment.

When I was inside I looked at the loot. The two diamonds

were all that I thought they were. They were worth enough to keep a man in the style anyone would like to become accustomed to. Then I looked at the box. It was still just a box and a pretty damned empty one. But now I could make a good guess about it. With spies and counterspies mixed up in it, there was a good chance that there was some secret writing on the box somewhere or some kind of paper still concealed in it. But I wasn't going to take a chance messing it up by looking for it when I didn't know what "it" was, exactly. I put the box and the diamonds away and went to bed.

The next morning, I called the office and told Peaches-and-Cream to tell Niels that I didn't feel well. She made a few cracks about hangovers before disconnecting. Then I sat down to wait.

I didn't have long to wait for the first call, the one I was expecting. The working day had barely started when the phone sounded off. I picked up the receiver and said hello.

"Milo, this is Lieutenant Malikoff," he said. He was being formal; we'd been calling each other Milo and Murray for years. That meant it was going the way I wanted it to go. "What's this about you being sick? I just called the office."

"Yeah," I said, yawning audibly. "To tell the truth, I'm not sick. It's just that I knew there weren't any cases in the office and I wanted to catch up on a little shut-eye. Didn't get too much sleep last night."

"Oh?" he said. I grinned, wondering if he had any idea how much like a cop he sounded. He tried to put the question casually. "Out working on a case?"

"No," I said. "Just a little old-fashioned pub crawling. You know how it is, Lieutenant. A brandy here and a brandy there, and before you know it the dawn is coming up like thunder out of China across the bay. And I do mean thunder."

"Uh-huh," he said, and you could tell he didn't believe it. "Ever hear of a guy named Dubinov?"

"You sure you don't mean Dubonnet?" I asked. "If that's what you mean, it's wine—and I never touch soft drinks. Lips that touch limeade shall never touch mine."

"You're pretty funny this morning," he growled. "But I mean Dubinov. The guy who was murdered last night."

"Goodness, Lieutenant," I said sweetly. I was needling him intentionally. "You mean one of our citizens was killed last night? I thought all that had stopped after you got on the force."

"Look," he said angrily, "we got a call about this murder last night. Sergeant Burns took the call. He's talked to you plenty of times and he swears it was your voice on the phone."

"Me? You know I never make anonymous phone calls."

Malikoff's voice was harder now. "This guy who was killed was a member of the NTS, the Russian underground movement. I've been talking to Merrick over at the FBI, and he tells me that you were in asking him what the NTS was. And you were asking him about thirty minutes before this call came in. What about that?"

"It just goes to show you what a small world it is," I exclaimed. "Here I was doing a crossword puzzle about the NTS just at the same time you were hearing about a real NTS puzzle. Now, ain't that a coincidence?"

"Yeah," he said dryly. He covered the mouthpiece of his

phone and talked with somebody. I could hear the murmur of his voice. I could even guess who the somebody was. It was probably Merrick, the FBI man.

"Look, Milo," he said, coming back on, "for the last time, are you going to play ball with us?"

"Lieutenant," I exclaimed, "I told you I was pub crawling last night. You don't honestly expect me to get out this early in the morning and start playing ball on some dew-covered lot?"

He said a short, hard word.

"Please, Lieutenant, the operator might be listening in, and I happen to know she's a sensitive girl."

"What the hell's come over you, Milo?" he demanded harshly. "It's not like you to refuse to cooperate at all. I asked at your office and I know you're not on a case, so whatever you're doing in this, you're in it on your own. That means your neck is way out, Milo."

"My neck isn't out," I said. "It's just these short collars I've been wearing lately."

I could hear another voice saying something. That was probably Merrick again.

"All right, Milo," said Lieutenant Malikoff. "If that's the way you want it—"

"That's the way I want it," I said, and beat him to it. I hung up first.

Unless I was wrong about Merrick, they'd work fast. I had one thing I wanted to do first. I called Arlene Denning and told her that I had her box. She gushed with gratitude and wanted to know how soon I could bring it over.

"I don't know," I said. "I'm going to be pretty busy all day here in my apartment, catching up on some reports I have to make. I can't do anything else until I've finished them. Then I'll have to make a report on the box to the office and to the police, and then I'll bring it over to you. Say this evening after dinner."

"The police?" she said. There was a long pause, and I had an idea that she, too, was carrying on a conversation with someone else. With Henri. "Must you go to the police?" she asked finally.

"Of course," I said. "There was a crime committed to get the box, even though you didn't report it. But we have to get along with the police, so we have to give them a report on everything. It won't hold anything up. It'll just be a routine thing. I'll be there this evening with it, don't worry. … You still keeping that light burning in the window for me, honey?"

It was obvious that her mind was more on what Henri was saying than on me. "Of course," she said uncertainly. "Well, all right … Milo." She hung up.

After that, it was mostly waiting. I made a few other calls, every thirty minutes. I found out what time planes for Los Angeles left, when I could catch a train to Washington, checked on the feature picture at three movie places, and found out the price of a new television set. It was on the last call that I finally heard what I'd been listening for. After that I didn't make any more calls. I just sat around having a few brandies and waited.

It was almost four o'clock that afternoon when the phone call came. It was Arlene Denning. This time she was really turning on the allure. She wanted to see me at once. Could she come to my apartment? For a minute I toyed with it, but then decided against it. I told her that I had a cleaning woman coming in.

"Then let me pick you up," she said. "I've got the car. We can go somewhere and have dinner together and then … just be alone."

"What about Henri?" I asked.

"Oh, he went away again," she said. She managed to get a pout in her voice. "To hell with Henri. Just you and me, Milo."

"I'd like that," I said.

"And bring the box."

"You forgot what I told you before," I said. "About the report."

"We'll do it together," she said. "Then we can go anywhere you like. To your place—or back here. George won't be home."

"Well … ," I said, sounding more eager.

"I'll pick you up in front of your place right away," she said. "What's the address?"

I gave it to her. My phone was unlisted, so I'd known that the only way she could get it was from me.

"I'll be there in fifteen minutes," she said. She laughed. "You won't be sorry, Milo." The phone clicked as she hung up.

I resisted the temptation to say something else and replaced the receiver. Then I started getting ready for my heavy date.

I had an old four-barreled derringer. It was a real old-timer and so small it would fit easily in the palm of my hand. The gunsmith had done some work on it and fixed it so it would fire regular bullets. I got it out and strapped it on my forearm against my side and baby would drop out of the clip and into my hand.

Then I put on my coat. I put the box in one pocket and the diamonds in the other pocket. I was about as complete a clay pigeon as you'd find in a long time.

When fifteen minutes were up, I went downstairs. She was just pulling into the curb. In a Cadillac. A lavender Cadillac. This was going to be in style.

"Hello, darling," she said. She leaned over and opened the door. Then, as I started to get in, she leaned a little farther and kissed me on the lips. There was nothing subtle about the kiss—or the neckline view I got in the process. She laughed as she took her lips away from mine and started the big car with a smooth lunge.

"This is our night, Milo," she said. This time her laugh sounded a little nervous. "You brought the box?"

"Sure, honey," I said easily. "Like you said, this is our night, and what kind of a night would it be without the box? The whole party would probably have to be called off while I went back after it."

She gave me a glance out of the corner of her eyes and there was flash of fear in them. Then came the other response I was waiting for. Something cold pressed against the back of my neck.

"All right, sucker," the voice said. I didn't have to turn around to know it was Henri. "This is a gun, so don't try anything."

"I wouldn't think of it," I said dryly. "I was wondering how soon you'd get tired of lying on the floor back there."

He called me something in French.

"You knew he was back there?" Arlene asked. I couldn't tell whether she sounded frightened or excited. It was probably both.

"It figured," I said. I sat rigidly still while Henri reached around and pulled my gun from its holster under my left arm. "The box is in my left coat pocket," I added.

He muttered something else and reached into my pocket. He came out with the box.

"No diamonds," he said. "Well, it doesn't really matter. The box is here. Perhaps we can get you to tell where the diamonds are."

"You mean those were really diamonds?" I said, laying it on thick. "I thought they were phonies and put them out with the garbage this morning."

He smacked me across the head with the gun. It wasn't hard enough to knock me out, but it hurt like hell.

"Don't be funny," he snapped. *"Chérie,* you remember which way we go?"

"I remember," she said. Her face was paler than usual. "Why did you do that, Henri? You promised me that nothing would happen to him. You said we'd just take the box and then leave him alone."

"We'll leave him alone—when we're through with him. Don't bother your pretty little head about it, *chérie.*"

"But—"

"No more," he said roughly. "You will do as you are told. More than that is not asked of you."

I felt a little sorry for Arlene; she was due for several more surprises before this was over.

We were driving north out of the city, and by this time we were almost to the city limits. There was a fair amount of traffic on the road, but there was no opportunity for me to do anything even if I'd wanted to. I didn't want to either.

Once we were across the city limits, the big Cadillac picked up speed. About two miles out, she swung to the right and drove up a narrow old road leading into the hills.

"Henri," she said, "there's a car following us." She sounded frightened.

"I know," he said. "Don't worry about it."

We drove another three miles without speaking. She turned into a graveled lane, and a few minutes later we stopped in front of an old, deserted-looking house. There wasn't another one in sight.

"Get out, *flic,*" Henri said, prodding the back of my neck with the gun. I seemed to remember that *flic* was an uncomplimentary French term for a cop, but I couldn't remember exactly what. However, this was hardly the time to worry about enlarging my bilingual abilities. I got out of the car.

"Inside," he said, prodding me some more. "Come on, Arlene. You're going with us."

"C-couldn't I just wait here?" she asked.

"No. Come on."

The three of us walked into the house. It was deserted, and from the looks of it, it had been for several years. It was still furnished, but everything was covered with layers of dust.

"M'sieu March," Henri said, "you can make it easy on your-self by telling me the whereabouts of the diamonds before the others arrive."

"No, thanks," I said dryly. "If I have to do any performing, I prefer to have a larger audience."

"Milo," Arlene Denning said, "I'm sorry about this. I didn't know anything about any diamonds. I thought he was only going to take the box away from you."

"Shut up," Henri said harshly.

"It's all right, honey," I told her. "I know you didn't know the score. I'm afraid, however, that Henri may teach it to you before we get out of here."

"It is better for you to shut up, too," Henri said, moving the gun to remind me.

There was the sound of another car pulling up outside. The doors slammed and a moment later the two men came in. Dimitri Monevsky and Lew Pisano, both of them looking mad. Lew had some adhesive on his jaw, and I suspected that Comrade Monevsky had some on his head under his hat.

"This is the guy?" Lew asked. He hadn't gotten a good look at me the night before.

"Yes," Monevsky said.

"I've been waiting for this moment," Lew said grimly. He started for me.

"Wait," Monevsky said sharply. "There is time enough for that. "What about the box?"

"I have it here," Henri said.

"Let me have it." Monevsky took the box and looked at it. "The false bottom is missing. That may be the piece we need."

"That wasn't in it when I got it," Lew Pisano said. "That guy last night, the one I bumped off, he'd whittled it up with a knife."

"Good," Monevsky said. "What we want must be here, then. What about the diamonds?"

"He didn't have them with the box." Henri answered. "I asked him about them, but he refuses to answer."

"Let me work him over," Lew said eagerly. "He'll talk."

"Maybe the three of you ought to draw straws," I said. "Or just try it all together—which would give you a better chance."

Monevsky nodded. "Shut him up," he said to Lew.

The latter had his gun out before the Russian stopped talking. He came at me with a grin. I tried to protect my face with my arms, but it wasn't much use. The heavy gun crashed right through my arms and caught me on the cheek.

It was then that Arlene Denning came back into the act. One thing I had to give her she had plenty of nerve.

"Henri," she said, "I don't know what this is about, but I'm leaving right now. And I suggest that you let Mr. March go, too." She started to walk past him.

Without even taking his eyes from me, Henri reached out and hit her with his open hand. It was enough to knock her sprawling on the floor.

"Stay here," he said viciously.

"You know, Henri," I said, "you really should introduce your friends to Arlene, so she'd know how to behave. And while you're at it, I suggest you introduce yourself and Comrade Monevsky to Lew Pisano. I have a hunch that he doesn't know how really important you are."

"What are you talking about?" Lew asked.

"Who do you think these two guys are, Lew?"

"A couple of boys from the East. Why?"

I laughed. "They're farther from the East than you think. Comrade Monevsky, who hired you to kill Alexis Dubinov—by the way, he did hire you, didn't he?"

"Yeah, but—"

"Well, Comrade Monevsky is an agent for Soviet Russia. I'm not sure about Comrade Ormont here, but I suspect he is someone fairly important in the French Communist Party. I'm not sure what that box contains, but it's something they want badly."

There was a gasp from Arlene, but her surprise was no greater than Lew Pisano's. He was looking suspiciously at the two men.

"Communists," he said. "I ain't so sure I like this. There's something kind of—I guess—un-American about it. ..."

Monevsky threw back his head and laughed. "There," he said, "is an excellent example of bourgeois attitude. It is all right to steal and murder, but it is un-American to give aid to the only genuine workers' state in the world."

"Don't worry, Lew," I said quickly. Maybe you're not a very good American, but I'd rather have you around than your two friends. You know, I've got an idea that you might get off with a manslaughter charge if you tell the truth about who hired you."

Monevsky drew a gun while Lew was still trying to decide which way to point his.

"Drop your gun," he said.

Lew hesitated a minute, then dropped it.

"Now move over beside March," Monevsky ordered. Lew obeyed.

"It is better this way," Monevsky said to Henri. "We do not need him anymore, and it is better that we leave behind no one who can give any information about us."

"I agree," Henri said. "It is also better for another reason. We can make it look as though Pisano kidnapped March and Arlene, and killed them when they tried to escape, getting killed in turn."

There was another gasp from the girl. Up until then, I think she'd believed this to be a rough party, but not that rough. Now she knew.

"Get it over with," Monevsky said.

"What about the diamonds?"

"We can search March and his apartment afterwards, but we must not risk what the box contains even for the diamonds. Kill them."

"With pleasure," Henri said. He leveled his gun on Lew Pisano.

I couldn't see the point of waiting an longer. Maybe I had figured this one too fine; it's bound to happen sometime. If so, it left me strictly on my own. I pressed my arm against my side and felt the derringer drop into my hand. It was like getting money from home.

Henri was just starting to squeeze the trigger when my bullet caught him right in the face. He looked awfully surprised in the brief second before it spoiled his good looks.

I didn't wait to admire the results. I swung, bringing the derringer to bear on Comrade Monevsky. And in that minute, the door burst open, and before either Monevsky or I could do anything, the place was filled with cops.

I took a deep breath—my first one in at least an hour—and slipped the derringer in my pocket. The cops knew exactly what they wanted, and they were on Monevsky and Lew Pisano like an early snowstorm.

Finally, strolling in behind the cops, came Lieutenant Malikoff, Merrick, the FBI man, and a third man I didn't recognize.

"Some rescue squad," I said. "You keep on drawing it this fine and I'll be liable to take my business elsewhere. Did you hear everything?"

"Almost," Malikoff said sourly. "What we missed Pisano can fill out, or you or Mrs. Denning. What do you mean by that crack about taking your business elsewhere?"

"You don't think I'd have set myself up as a clay pigeon if I hadn't known you guys had my wire tapped and would be Dick Tracying right after us?"

"How'd you know your phone was tapped?" Merrick asked.

"I know how a cop's mind works," I said with a grin. "I goaded you into doing something, and you being suspicious of me, that would be the first thing you'd think of doing. So I kept checking on the phone and listening until I heard that old familiar click, and then I knew it was all right to fall into the trap. Only next time, get here quicker."

The two of them looked at me. "Very cute," Malikoff said sourly. "Someday, Milo, you'll be too cute."

"Very childish," the FBI man said. "Why the hell didn't you just turn over what you had?"

"Because I didn't have anything," I said promptly. "I could have testified that Lew killed the underground agent, but that was all. This way you caught them all red-handed."

"And one of them red-faced," Malikoff said, glancing at Henri.

"Pardon me," said the third man. "The box?"

Merrick looked at me. I nodded toward Monevsky, who was being held by a couple of cops. Merrick went over and got the box out of the Russian's pocket. He handed it to the third man.

His hands trembled as he got out a knife and went to work on the box. One of the sides split, and he took from between the thin boards several tiny strips of film.

"They are still here," he said with relief.

"Look," I said, "I'm only the guy that broke this and delivered the whole thing to you on a platter. Now, will somebody tell me what the hell this is about?"

The FBI man and the third man exchanged glances.

"I guess you can tell him," the FBI man grunted. He glanced at me. "This is Ivan Lyshenko. He is also from the NTS, the Russian underground. He flew here today from Washington after the chief got in touch with him."

The third man smiled at me. "It is simple," he said. "The pearl necklace which Mrs. Denning purchased in Paris came from Russia. One of our men worked in the place that exported the necklace and he built the box. In it, he placed two diamonds and a number of microfilms showing atomic installations in Russia. He sent word to our organization in France. Our man went at once to the jewelry store, but Mrs. Denning had already purchased the necklace."

"The man who tried to buy it from me," exclaimed Arlene.

Precisely," said the NTS man. "In the meantime, the man who had done this had been arrested. Evidently, under torture, he talked. So the French Communist Party also sent a man around to get it. This was the man you know as Henri Ormont. He also discovered that Mrs. Denning had purchased the necklace. So he managed to come to America with Mrs. Denning. Of course, Monevsky was sent along to be sure that the proper results were obtained."

"That reminds me," the FBI man said, looking at me again. "What about the diamonds?"

"Diamonds?" I asked. I'd been thinking about them, too. Now I had an idea.

"There were two diamonds in the box concealed beneath the false bottom," the third man said. "They are very valuable stones, with a long history in Russia. Once they were known as the Czar's Tears—more recently they have been called Stalin's Tears. They were, of course, stolen from a state collection and sent along to help finance our organization. You have not seen them?"

"Diamonds, huh?" I said. I looked innocently at the FBI man. "Tell me something. Suppose I had found those diamonds. It looks to me like you would have to take custody of them, just like I'm sure you're taking custody of those microfilms. But the diamonds are different. We're still doing diplomatic business with Russia. They might be able to claim the diamonds as stolen property and we might have to return them."

The FBI man was trying to read my mind. "You're probably right," he said. "What about it?"

"It's a shame the underground has to lose all that financing," I said. "I got an idea. Maybe you ought to search the car Monevsky and Lew came in. Maybe they got the diamonds there."

Monevsky started to say something, but one of the cops shut him up. The FBI man just continued to stare at me.

"Milo is pretty childish," Malikoff said gruffly, "but sometimes he has a good ideas. Let's go search the car."

The FBI man took some more time making up his mind, but finally he nodded. They turned to go. Malikoff ordered the cops to take the two prisoners out. Then he turned to the NTS man.

"I want to keep the prisoners well guarded," he said gravely. "I guess there's no reason to hold Mr. March any longer, but would you keep an eye on him for a moment?"

The NTS man wasn't too sure what was going on, but he nodded. We all stood like wooden Indians while the cops marched out. When they were gone, I walked over and handed the two diamonds to the NTS agent. He understood then and grinned.

"Come on, Arlene," I said. "Your husband will think I'm keeping you out late."

One thing I had to say for that dame; she recovered quickly. By the time we walked into her house she'd completely gotten over her grief about Henri. She insisted that I come in for a drink, and I finally agreed to have a brandy.

We walked into the small study where I'd first seen her. She poured me a brandy and I drank it. When I set the glass down, she was standing right in front of me. Close.

"I haven't thanked you yet, Milo," she said.

"As it turned out," I said, "I didn't get your box back to you, so you don't owe me any thanks."

"Oh, but I do. If not for what you've already done, Milo, let's say ... for what you may do in the future."

She lifted her head and pressed her mouth against mine. He lips were like living fire. Her body, pressed tightly against mine, was like a poem in Braille.

After a moment, I pushed her away, took my handkerchief, and rubbed my lips.

"What's wrong, Milo?" she asked.

"There was a time," I said slowly, "when I was a kid, that I would take anything that was thrown me and no questions asked. But I've gotten older and more particular. I don't know what it is that's pushing you over, but it isn't me. I haven't got a thing you need—but a psychiatrist might have. Why don't you try that?"

I turned and walked out of the room—just ahead of the brandy glass, which shattered on the door as I closed it.

5

The Red, Red Flowers

It was one of those mornings when nothing was going right. I reached the office early because I was expecting a phone call. It still hadn't come. The mail hadn't been delivered, so I was reading the morning paper. The Giants had lost the day before. The Yankees had won a doubleheader from Boston. When it's that kind of day, everything goes wrong. In disgust, I turned to the front pages. Things weren't any better there. The Russians had caught a second U-2 pilot and his plane, and were promising a quick trial for the pilot.* I put the paper down and stared malignantly at the phone that didn't ring.

The name is March. Milo March. I'm an insurance investigator. At least that's what it says on my license and on the door of my Madison Avenue office. Which means that if you kill your wife, hoping to collect her insurance to spend on that blonde you met the other night, I'll probably be around looking for you. That's the general idea anyway. But everyone

---

* The first was the famous incident of May 1, 1960, when a U-2 was shot down and the pilot, Captain Francis Gary Powers, was captured. The second incident in this story published in 1961 (probably written in 1960) is fictional. The real second U-2 incident occurred during the Cuban Missile Crisis on October 27, 1962, when Major Rudolf Anderson, Jr., was shot down and killed.

must have been on a temporary goodness jag. I hadn't had a job in two weeks.

The mail arrived. All bills. So it was still the same kind of day. Then the door opened and there was another mailman, this one with a registered letter. I signed for it and he went away. I opened the letter and the day was complete. It said that Major March, U.S. Army Reserve, was recalled to active duty. I was to report to an address in Washington. It was that same day. The time was sixteen hundred, or four o'clock. Which meant that I had about six in which to make it.

I thought of ignoring the whole thing, pretending I had never gotten the letter. But it had been registered, and when the Army wants you, they only give you two choices. You can walk in or be dragged in. So I made arrangements with another investigator to handle anything that came in for me, and notified my answering service to route the calls to him. Then I went downtown to my apartment in Greenwich Village. I dug out my uniform and discovered it didn't need anything but a pressing. I took it into the tailor, and went to the Blue Mill for a couple of martinis while being pressed.

At two o'clock that afternoon, looking every inch the well-dressed Army officer, I was at LaGuardia Field boarding a plane for Washington. An hour later I was telling a Washington cab driver where to take me, but I didn't give him the address in the orders, but a street corner nearby. When I got out of the cab I still had about a half hour to spare. I spent it in the nearest gin mill over another martini. I believe that Regulations state that an officer shouldn't drink while on duty, but then I wouldn't really be on duty until after I reported. Finally I walked down the street, looking for the address. There were three vacant lots in the middle of the block where builders had just begun to excavate. Beyond them were several old brownstone houses of the type which in recent years have been taken over by government bureaus. I walked past the vacant lots and reached the first building. I looked at the number. It was too high. I turned and retraced my steps. But after a few steps I realized that the number in my orders, if it had ever existed, had been where one of the vacant lots was now. I cursed to myself. If I'd had any doubts before about who was responsible for my return to active duty, they were gone.

I heard steps on the sidewalk while I was still standing there with the orders in my hand. I looked around. A pleasant-faced young man was strolling toward me. I almost ignored him, but then I took another look. There was something a little too studied about his casualness, and I knew I was right. I turned back to the vacant lot and stared at it innocently.

"Pardon me, Major," the young man said as he reached me, "is there anything wrong?"

I turned my innocence on him. "Why," I said, "I seem to have been given the wrong address."

"Perhaps I can help you," he said. "I know the neighborhood rather well. What address are you looking for?" He moved in slightly behind me as though to look over my shoulder. Out of the corner of my eye, I caught a slight movement of his right arm and I heard the scrape of something against cloth.

"This one," I said, holding up the paper.

I knew that the movement would catch his eyes for at least a couple of seconds. I lifted my left foot and brought it down hard on his right instep. There was a gasp of pain from him. I dropped the paper and pivoted, sending a right to his stomach just hard enough to bend him over. I chopped across his neck with the edge of my left hand and he dropped. He was unconscious—which was the way I wanted him. A slender blackjack was lying on the sidewalk next to him. I left him and the blackjack where they had fallen. I picked up my orders, folded the paper, and put it back in my pocket. Fortunately the street was still empty, so there was no one to raise a cry about the man on the street. I walked back to the first house beyond the lots. It seemed like the logical place.

This time I looked in. There was a tiny vestibule with an inner door, but there were no mailboxes, nameplates, or bells in it. Beyond the second door, I could see a long corridor with doors on either side. About halfway down the corridor there was a soldier, obviously standing guard. I could have just gone in and presented my orders and he probably would have escorted me into the office. But I was sore and I didn't want it that way.

I stepped back out on the street. The young man was still lying on the sidewalk. I skirted around the side of the brownstone and went to the back. There was a parking area there with four cars in it. One was an Army car with three stars on it. That proved I was right.

I hunted around the back until I found a greasy cloth that had been used on one of the cars. I slipped up to the rear door

and tried it. It was locked, but it took me only a moment to pick it. I opened the door just enough to slip the rag, bunched up, in between it and the sill at the bottom. I struck a match and held it to the cloth. As soon as it began to smolder, I hurried back to the front of the house. I slipped into the vestibule, against the wall, and watched the soldier on guard. After a few seconds he began to sniff and look around. He caught a glimpse of smoke trickling in through the back door and hurried toward it.

The minute he moved, I had the second door open and was going quietly down the hall behind him. He was bending over the burning rag as I reached the door he'd been guarding. I opened the door silently and stepped inside. I was in a small, empty office. There was an open door leading into another, larger office. There were voices coming from that other office.

"I don't see why you had to do it this way," a man was saying. "We know March's work well enough. Why didn't you just have him come straight here and get it over with?"

"I like to test men before I give them assignments," said another voice. It was one I knew all too well. He chuckled. "O'Connor should be here with him any minute. It'll be worth a lot to see March's face when he comes here in the office."

I lit a cigarette and went to stand in the doorway. "You don't have to wait that long," I said. "Take a good look now."

The three men in the room whirled to look at me. I knew all three of them. One of them was George Hillyer, the civilian head of the Central Intelligence Agency. The other civilian was Philip Emerson, his assistant. And the third man was a big, red-faced Army officer with three bright shining stars on his collar. Lieutenant General Sam Roberts. The two civilians were quickly over their surprise, and I noticed they were both grinning but being careful to hide the fact from the General. He was still staring at me with his mouth open, but his face was beginning to get redder.

"Old Tricky Roberts," I said. "You haven't changed since the days when you couldn't steal a chicken without being caught." During the fracas that was known as World War II, General Roberts and I had been in OSS together, working behind the German lines. But he'd been a colonel then.

"You're talking to a superior officer, Major March," the

General said. His voice was as stiff as an overstarched collar. "I could break you for that."

"Anyone who'll talk to a superior officer ought to be broken," I retorted. "Don't give me that malarkey, General. I know you since you were a chicken colonel, polishing those eagles until they screamed. You're in trouble, or I wouldn't have been recalled to active duty. You break me and who'll pull your chestnuts from the fire?"

His face was a deep purple. "Silence," he roared. "How the hell did you get in here? O'Connor—" He broke off. "Anyway, Sanders was just outside the door with orders not to let anyone in," he finished.

There was an interruption. The outer door opened and two men came into the office. The first one was the soldier who had been on guard. He was followed by the young man I'd met in the street. He was limping and rubbing his neck.

"I beg your pardon, General," the soldier said, "but the back door was unlocked and somebody had stuffed an oily rag in it and set it on fire. But I didn't see anybody around."

The General glared at me and I gave him a sweet smile. He swung back to the two men. "What kind of an outfit is this?" he said angrily. "Can't anyone carry out a simple order without fouling it up?"

"The only one who's goofed around here," I said, "is a certain three-star general. First you send me orders with a phony address on them. Then you send a pet bird dog out to point me into a trap. Just so you can get a belly laugh when I'm dragged in by the heels."

"Well," the General said lamely, "I just wanted to see if

civilian life had softened you up." He glanced at the two men in the doorway. "How about it, O'Connor?"

It was the young man who answered. "I'd say it hadn't, sir. I was in back of him, but I never had a chance."

"All right, go home, O'Connor. Take a couple of days off. Sanders, go back and wait in the car for me." The General swung his gaze back to me. "So right away you come in and beat up one of my best men, then you pick the lock on the back door, shove in a burning rag—which could have burned down the building—to draw away the guard just so you can make a grandstand play by breaking in here?"

"You want to play games," I said, "that's what you'll get. You never saw the day you could outsmart me. You tried it plenty of times when we were behind the lines together."

Any mention of the war always relaxed him. He leaned back in his chair and beamed at me. "It was a great war, wasn't it, Milo?"

"Save it for your memoirs," I said. "What kind of trouble are you in that you have to drag me back into this monkey suit?"

"You're right about its being trouble, Major," George Hillyer said. "The three of us discussed it and decided you were the best man for the job. ... Yesterday the Russians got another of our U-2 planes."

"I read about it in the paper this morning," I said. "I thought those were the planes that flew so high no one could shoot them down. Do the Russians have a new type of gun?"

"No," the General growled. "The first plane had a jet flame-out and went down to thirty thousand feet. They couldn't have touched him at seventy thousand. The second plane had gone down to twenty thousand feet, under orders, when the Russians hit his plane."

"Why so low?"

"To make a drop," Hillyer said. "The pilot was supposed to drop ammunition, money, and information to a resistance group inside Russia. They got him before he succeeded in making the drop."

"What does this have to do with me?" I asked.

It was Hillyer who answered. "You've heard of Narodno Trudovoi Soyuz, Major?"

I nodded. "The National Alliance of Russian Solidarists. It's a group of anti-Communist Russians."

"Right. Their headquarters are in West Germany, but they have thousands of agents inside Russia. No one but Russians are permitted in the group. They have been very successful, mostly because of what they call the molecule system. It's something like the old Communist cell. Each group of agents in Russia consists of three persons, and those three do not know any other group. If one is captured and tortured, he can only inform on two other members. These NTS people have been very valuable to us in providing information. In return we have supplied them with money and materials. Our pilot was making a drop to an American agent in Russia who was then to contact a number of these underground molecules."

"Wasn't it dangerous having a man there who knew the different groups?"

"He didn't know them. The drop included a coded message to him giving him the location of the groups. The message was concealed behind a map of Russia, which would be part of a regular U-pilot's equipment. If anything had happened to the plane and pilot, we wanted the Russians to think it was a regular flight."

"Did they?"

"So far they have. But the map is one of the things they have on display in the Hall of Columns in Moscow.* And the pilot knows there's a message on the back of the map. We don't believe he's being brainwashed or anything like that, but there's always a chance that he may try to use the information during his trial or later in prison to make a trade. If the Russians get the message, hundreds of agents will die, and we will lose a valuable source of information."

I was beginning to get the idea and I didn't like it. "You mean you want the pilot and the message snatched out of the Russians' hands?"

"Exactly."

"I could smell that one coming," I said. "I don't like it. You know, I've been in East Germany twice and Russia once.** They have my fingerprints and considerable information about me. It won't be easy even to get into the country."

"We have that problem licked," the General said. It was the first time he'd spoken for several minutes.

"How?"

"It is not yet known," he said, "but we have a U-3 plane. Same as the U-2 but it will carry two men. We fly you over

---

* The Hall of Columns (or Pillar Hall) is a ballroom in the House of the Unions, a historic building once used by the Russian nobility and later taken over by the Communists for State functions, including trials against Stalin's enemies in the 1930s.

** See the M.E. Chaber novels *No Grave for March*, *The Splintered Man*, and *So Dead the Rose*.

Russia at seventy thousand feet and you parachute in. Perfectly safe."

"For everybody except me," I said.

"It's fairly safe," Hillyer said. "We have a few days' time. We're going to have you brush up on your Russian and see that you get all the other information you need. We're providing you with clothes and identification, everything you need to prove that you're a Russian. We know you speak Russian well enough to fool them. We can give you one more bit of help. There will be one underground molecule—that is, three persons—who will assist you and be under your orders. For the rest you will be on your own."

"From fourteen miles up in the air?" I said. "That's really being on your own."

When the Army gets an idea, that's it. You'd think ideas were invented at West Point. Anyway, it went the way they said. I spent the next several days polishing my Russian. I took special classes each day and even went to sleep at night plugged into sleep lessons. In between I was fitted out for a pressure suit for the parachute jump, and given a complete set of clothes that had been made in Russia. I was given all kinds of identification cards, including a Party card and proof that I was a worker from Rostov who was spending two weeks in Moscow. I was even provided with a short-handled shovel, to bury the pressure suit after I landed; the shovel also had been made in Russia. Five days after reporting for duty, I was on an Army plane headed for Pakistan.

Three more days went by after we landed there.

I was introduced to the pilot who would fly me over

Russia—a tall, blond boy from Indiana—and stuffed into a pressure suit. I felt, and probably looked, like an invader from Mars. I was led out to the plane, a stubby-winged, sleek-looking black plane with a needle nose. I climbed into the rear seat and hooked my helmet into the intercom. I checked to be sure that I had the knapsack that was going to parachute in with me.

"You plugged in, Major?" the pilot asked. His voice coming through the earphones in the helmet had a hollow sound.

"I seem to be," I said.

"All set, Major?"

"As much as I'll ever be," I grunted. "But I have a feeling that this is one thing which will never become habit-forming with me."

"There's nothing to it," he said cheerfully. "You don't even have to pull a ripcord. Your chute will open automatically when you've fallen about eight miles."

"They didn't tell me that jokes were a part of this, or I wouldn't have come," I said. "Where are you dropping me?"

"About ten miles southeast of Moscow. That'll give you the rest of the night to walk into the city."

"How can you be sure that's where you'll drop me?"

"Major, in this weather, I could drop you from this height and make you land on a dime. I don't even have to do any guessing about it. The whole thing's worked out mathematically."

We flew along in silence the next few minutes. Then he spoke again. "Better start getting ready, Major. Be sure you've got everything you want to take with you. It's hard coming back after something you forgot. There's a lever in front of you. See it?"

"Yeah."

"When I tell you to go, disconnect your communication cord and pull that lever. It'll drop you through the bottom of the ship and you'll be on your way. Okay?"

"Okay," I muttered, but I wasn't sure it was. I felt the way I had the first time I had a serious date with a girl—light-headed. I checked to be sure the knapsack was fastened to my shoulders. I would have liked to check the rest of my equipment but I didn't know anything about it, so I waited.

"Go ahead, Major," the pilot said quietly. "And good luck."

"Thanks," I said. I reached up and pulled the cord from my helmet. I took a deep breath and pushed the lever in front of me.

After what seemed a very long time, I felt the tug of the parachute as it opened. After that, I was vaguely aware of swinging like a pendulum from it, but it was a pleasant sensation. Then, almost before I knew it, the ground came up to meet me and I went tumbling across it until the chute collapsed. I managed to unbuckle it and then take my helmet off. There was a gentle breeze and the smell of earth, but there were no lights.

I rested for a couple of minutes, then took the knapsack off my back. I removed my gloves and opened the pack. There was a small flashlight at the very top. Shielding the light, I looked around. I was in the middle of a plowed field.

I took the other clothes from the knapsack, and quickly undressed and put them on. I took the shovel and dug a hole in the field. I gathered up the parachute and folded it, dropping it and the pressure suit into the hole. I checked the knapsack to be sure that everything was out of it, then dropped it in too and shoveled the dirt back. When I was sure that the spot looked like the rest of the field, I used the light to check my compass and headed off in the direction of Moscow. About a mile on the way, I threw the shovel into a ditch, after first wiping the handle clean so there would be no fingerprints on it.

It was just four o'clock in the morning when I approached the edge of the city. I had already decided it would be foolish to start marching through the streets at that hour in the morning, so I found a field with some bushes in it and curled up and went to sleep.

It was shortly after eight when I awakened. Now there was some traffic on the road, mostly trucks. No one paid any attention to me as I walked into the city. I soon reached a bus stop, where several workers were waiting for a bus, and I joined them. I was dressed a little better than the other men— because I was, after all, on my vacation—but no one looked at me twice. I rode the bus into the center of Moscow and began to breath a little easier.

It didn't take me long to find the address I'd been given. It was one of the new apartment buildings on the Kotelnicheskaye Embankment. It was in block D, entrance C. I worked my way through the corridors until I found the apartment. I knocked on the door and hoped someone was home.

The door was opened by a girl. She was small, dark-haired, and pretty. Even the loose-fitting clothes couldn't conceal that she had a full figure.

"Dobroe utro," I said. *"U vas est mesto dlae mene?"* It was part of a recognition code.

"Prikhodite v luboe vremae," she answered. "It is lovely in Moscow this time of year."

"Yes," I said. "I have been admiring the red, red flowers that grow around the Kremlin."

She smiled and stepped back, opening the door wider. "Come in," she said.

I entered the apartment and she closed the door. I looked around. There were two rooms, small but attractive. I turned back to the girl.

"We were expecting you today," she said. "I am Natasha Naristova."

"I'm Milo March," I said, "but here I will be known as Mikhail Mikhailovich." I showed her my identification.

"It is well done," she said, after looking at the papers. "You had no trouble in finding the apartment?"

"No. I've been in Moscow before."

"I know," she said. "I remember reading about the capitalist spy Milo March. But your country proved that you couldn't have been here, didn't they?"

I nodded. "Do you live here alone?"

"No, with my brother. He is one of us. He is at work now."

"You don't work?"

"Oh, yes. I am on the staff of *Pravda.* This is my day off. What are your plans? All we were told was to expect an agent, and to give him any help he needed."

"I want to go to the opening of the trial of the American

pilot tomorrow. I have to get him and part of his possessions out of the country. Both are a threat to your group."

"That will be difficult," she said gravely. "I do not see how it can be done by only four of us."

"I will try to do most of it myself," I told her. "I don't want to risk you more than I have to."

"We will do what is needed. Tonight the third member of our group will be here and it can be discussed. You will stay here as long as you need to. Is there anything you would like now?"

"Some sleep," I said. "I had only three or four hours in a field this morning."

She led the way into the second room and indicated the two beds. I stretched out on one and was soon asleep.

I was awake by the middle of the afternoon. The girl was in the other room, reading. She made tea, and we spent the rest of the afternoon talking. At about five o'clock, her brother arrived. He was a big, blond fellow about my own age. His name was Ilya. He seemed even more pleased than his sister to learn that I was an American agent. During dinner, which Natasha cooked, he plied me with questions about America.

Shortly after dinner, there was a knock on the door. Ilya went and opened it. The man who entered was short and dark, with what seemed to be a perpetually scowling face. He was introduced to me as the third member of their NTS molecule. His name was Yuri Mogilev. Natasha brought out a bottle of vodka and filled four glasses. When they were passed around, she lifted her own.

"To a free Russia," she said, and we all drank. Then she

brought out a chessboard and set it up between her brother and Yuri. They began to put the pieces on the board.

"We always bring out the chessboard," Natasha said. "Everyone believes that is the reason Yuri visits us so often. So if anyone comes while we are having a meeting, there is only a chess game."

The men moved the pieces around a few times and then settled back. "Now," said Ilya, "we are ready to discuss your problems. You have papers?"

I nodded. "I am Mikhail Mikhailovich, from Rostov. There I am a minor clerk in the offices of Internal Affairs. I have a two weeks' vacation, which I am spending in Moscow. I have all the necessary papers."

"Good. You will stay here, of course. If there are any questions, you and I were in the army together and that is why you are visiting me." He turned to Yuri. "You know the American pilot who goes on trial tomorrow? The task is to get him out of the country."

Yuri pursed his lips and scowled even more. "It is a big order. They will make the most of him for propaganda, and he will be well guarded. You have a plan?"

I shook my head. "I'll try to make it up as I go along. Will I have any trouble getting into the trial tomorrow?"

"No. That will be open to the public."

"Do any of you know where the pilot is being held prisoner?"

Ilya glanced at Yuri, who nodded. "The Voldovna Prison. It is where they take important political prisoners before their trials."

"Can I get any sort of rough plan of the prison, and the location of the pilot's cell?"

"I can get that for you," Ilya said. "By tomorrow night, I think. Anything else?"

"I don't think so. ... I have considerable money with me, most of it in American dollars. I'll probably need to spend most of it in getting out. Will the dollars be better for bribes?"

"I do not think so," Ilya said. "I think you should change the dollars in the black market. Yuri can take care of it."

The four of us sat up talking late into the night, mostly about America, before we finally went to sleep. When I awakened the next morning I was alone in the apartment. There was a note from Natasha telling me where to find things for breakfast and how to get to the Hall of Columns. I had some rolls and tea, and left.

A crowd was already gathering for the trial. I entered the building with three or four others dressed pretty much as I was. Out in the corridor, there was a long, glass-covered case and a uniformed MVD man on guard. We filed by and looked at the things that had been taken from the captured pilot. There were a good many guns with ammunition, several watches, a big stack of ruble notes, a small bottle with a card identifying it as poison, all of the pilot's personal things, and the map. The latter was all I was interested in. Under the guise of gaping at the collection, I studied the case. It was locked as well as being guarded.

I followed the others into the large room that had once been the grand ballroom of the old Noblemen's Club, where the trial was to be held. It was flooded with lights, and there were several television cameras set up. About half the room was filled with newspapermen, many of them from the Western countries, including America. Fortunately, I didn't see any who might recognize me. Not that they might anyway, for this was going to be a big show and all eyes would be riveted on it.

The trial was quickly called to order, and the prosecutor faced the prisoner. "What is your name?" he asked.

"James Cooper," he said when the question had been translated into English.

"What is your nationality?"

"American."

"What is your profession?"

"Pilot."

There followed the reading of a long indictment of his crimes against the Soviet Union. I breathed a little easier when I realized that it contained no mention of his intending to contact the underground. It did list the guns and ammunition but merely charged that he'd had them in case of crashing inside Russia. When the indictment was finished, Cooper asked how he pleaded.

"Guilty," he said in a firm voice.

Lieutenant General Borisoglebsky, the presiding judge, leaned forward. "Weren't you aware that flying over Russia was a hostile act?" he asked.

"I didn't think about it," Cooper said.

"Didn't you realize your action might bring about a war?"

"Things like that were for the people who sent me to worry about."

And so it went throughout the day, the questions and

answers droning on evenly. Cooper wasn't volunteering any information, although it seemed to me that he was being more cooperative than he had to be. But then, he may have been ordered to do so in case of capture.

Ilya and Natasha were already at the apartment when I got there. We had dinner together, and shortly afterwards Yuri arrived. He brought a newspaper with him and we took turns reading the story of that day's trial. They were milking it for everything they could.

Ilya had brought a hand-drawn map of Voldovna Prison, with the location of Cooper's cell marked on it. I examined it carefully, but the more I looked at it, the more impossible the job seemed. There were three outer doors to penetrate before reaching the cell blocks, and each one of those doors was locked and guarded.

"It looks difficult," I admitted finally.

"I think it is impossible," Natasha said. She'd been leaning over my shoulder, looking at the map with me. "We are told that even a regular visitor, with an official pass to visit a prisoner, must go through questioning by the three guards, and each guard communicates with the next one before you pass through the door. It is almost certain that they will be even more careful with an American prisoner."

"The biggest problem is time," I muttered. "How long do you suppose the trial will last?"

"Exactly two more days," Natasha said.

"Exactly? How do you know that?" I wondered.

"The hall is reserved for only two more days. And the writers and cameramen from *Pravda* are assigned for that time.

They already have other assignments for the third day from now."

"At least it lets us know how much time we have," I said. "There is one other way. I don't like it, but maybe we have no choice. Ilya, is there any way we can get complete details on the transportation of Cooper to and from the trial? I mean routes, time, method of taking him and the number of guards."

"I think so," he said slowly. "There is a man with whom I sometimes play chess at lunchtime. He would know, and I think he could be bribed."

"I'll give you the money," I said. "Try to get it tomorrow. Can you take extra time at lunch or take the afternoon off?"

"I can take the afternoon off."

"Then bring whatever you get here, and I'll meet you. There are a couple of other things I want to ask you about, but first there is something I want to do. I'll be back soon."

"Where are you going?" Natasha asked.

"Out," I said with a smile.

"Let me go with you," she said. "I can be of help."

"Not this time," I told her firmly. "I'll be back within an hour." I smiled at her and left.

It was still early in the evening, but there wasn't much traffic. I hit the small side streets and began walking and looking. I'd been searching for more than a half hour before I found what I was looking for. I was on a narrow, dimly lit street. There were two or three small restaurants and a few shops along it, and the rest were apartment houses. There was a man walking ahead of me; as he reached a streetlight I saw he was wearing an MVD uniform.* I quickened my step.

I timed it carefully so as not to get too near until he was in between streetlights. He started to cross a narrow street angling off to the left, and I hurried forward.

"Comrade," I called, just loud enough to reach him but not enough to attract the attention of anyone in the apartment houses.

He hesitated and looked back, peering at me. "What is it?" he called. He sounded irritable.

"I need help," I said. I was almost up to him.

"I am off duty," he said, his tone clearly indicating that he didn't want to be bothered.

"It will take only a minute," I said. I reached him and looked around. There was no one on the street within two blocks of us. "It is only that I need some advice about something I found on the street."

"What is it?" he asked.

I reached into my pocket and pulled out a piece of paper. I held it out. "This," I said.

He took the paper and held it up, trying to get enough light on it to see it. I chopped my hand across his neck as hard as I could. He grunted deep in his throat and started to fall. I caught him and dragged him into the deep shadows of the alley. I went back to retrieve the paper I'd handed him. Then I went back and quickly stripped off his uniform. I rolled it up into a ball with the gun inside, and tucked the whole thing under my arm. It had taken no more than three or four

---

* The MVD is the Ministerstvo Vnutrennikh Del (Ministry of Internal Affairs), the Soviet agency of secret police, intelligence, and internal security.

minutes, and he was still unconscious as I stepped back to the street and walked away.

The uniform looked like any bunch of clothes under my arm, and I didn't draw a second glance from any of the few people I met on the way back to the apartment. Even so, I felt better when Natasha opened the door in answer to my knock. I stepped inside and she closed the door.

"I am glad you are back," she said. "What do you have there?"

I unrolled the uniform and smiled at the surprise on all three faces.

"What is it for?"

"I also have to do something to repatriate that paper Cooper was carrying before they find out about it. That comes before anything else tomorrow. I won't need help. This will either work simply and quickly—or not at all. Let's return to the second operation. If Ilya can get the information tomorrow, I will need two things. One will be easy, the other not."

"What do you want, Milo?" Natasha asked quietly.

"First, some old clothes. They should be working clothes, and the older the better."

"We have some of Ilya's that should fit you," Natasha said.

"Any way they could be traced to him if anything happens?" I asked.

She shook her head. "They came from the government store here, and there must be millions like them in Russia."

"All right. Now the hard one. I want to know where I can steal a car. But not any car. This should be old one that looks as if it's about fall apart. Maybe the kind of car that a man who was a good mechanic could recover from a junk heap and fix up."

"That's Yuri's department," Ilya said.

The short, dark man was lost in thought for a minute. Then he smiled. It was only the second time I'd seen him smile. "I know just the car," he said. "It would even be well if it were traced later, for the man who owns it is an informer on his neighbors. I can steal it any evening."

"Tomorrow evening? Or tomorrow afternoon?"

He scowled. "Tomorrow evening for certain. Perhaps in the afternoon. Sometimes he is home by three o'clock."

"All right," I said. "We'll see what happens. Everything will depend on the information Ilya gets tomorrow. If it looks possible, then tomorrow afternoon you will show me where the car is, and I will steal it and make the try."

"If you try to rescue the pilot tomorrow," Natasha said, "what do we do?"

"You will have already done it," I told her. "The plans, the car, advice, that's about it."

They all three started to protest.

"Wait," I said. "I was sent to do this job. The way I'm planning it, everything will have a better chance if I do it alone. More people would only make them suspicious and we might even get in each other's way. And there's another thing. The three of you have important work to do here. My orders are to use your assistance as much as I have to, but not to risk you unduly. But there is one other thing you can be putting your minds to."

"What?"

"If I succeed in rescuing Cooper, I'll need someplace to hide him until we can make a break for it."

"We could keep him here," Natasha said.

I shook my head. "Too dangerous, unless we have no choice. It should be somewhere else."

"There might be another place," she said. "There is a girl I know slightly, who has a one-room apartment on the next floor. She is away on vacation now. If we could get into her apartment in some way …"

"I can get in," I said. "So that's settled."

"But how will you get him out of Russia?" Ilya asked.

I grinned. "More theft," I said. "My idea is to try to get to some field where we can steal a plane. A fast one. Then Cooper can fly us out. It's risky, but probably safer than anything else. Once I've gotten him, you can be sure of one thing—the bloodhounds will be over every inch of Russia."

"I like the way you think," Yuri exclaimed. "Perhaps I could go with you."

"No, Yuri," I said. "Your job is here, and, believe me, it's a much tougher one."

"Milo is right, Yuri," Natasha said.

"But in the meantime," I said, "you can be thinking about where we might have the best chance of getting a plane, and the best way to reach it."

Yuri nodded, trying not to show his disappointment.

We talked generally for another hour or so, then Yuri left, and the three of us went to sleep.

I was up early the next morning, and back at the trial as soon as the building was open. While I was waiting for everyone to file into the trial room, I took another look at the case the MVD man was guarding. The map was still there. I didn't want to attract attention by too much interest in the case, so I strolled around the building. There were several offices around at the other end of it, mostly filled with either MVD men or what seemed to be Russian VIPs. I got a couple of questioning glances and soon retreated to the trial room.

The hearing was much the same as the day before. It was clear that they were more bent on making the United State look guilty than in bringing out anything on Cooper.

Just before the midday recess, the defense attorney got up to answer one of the prosecutor's blasts. He painted a glowing picture of Cooper as a simple Midwestern boy, with an honest, peace-loving family, who never knew what he was getting into. He said that these were the kind of Americans the Russians understood and liked. And he wound up by saying, "To show the world the true meaning of socialist humanitarianism, this boy's father and two brothers are on their way to Russia right now as guests of the government. They will arrive in Moscow tonight, and be here by his side tomorrow when he once more faces this court."

There was a burst of applause from the audience, and then court was adjourned until afternoon. I hurried back to the apartment. Ilya was already there. To my surprise, so was Natasha.

"I decided to take the afternoon off, too," she explained. "It is not difficult in my job."

I nodded and turned to Ilya. "How did you make out?"

"Fine," he said. He brought a piece of paper from his pocket. "But it cost fifteen thousand rubles."

"It's worth it," I said. "Let's see."

The three of us bent over the sheet of paper. Ilya had made a crude drawing of the route between the prison and the Hall of Columns, with all the streets marked. The time of departure, both morning and afternoon, was written down, and the other information I had wanted. He was transported in an official MVD car with three guards, one of whom drove. The driver was an MVD man, and the other two were KGB. That made it a little tougher, but it still looked possible.

"I think I can do it," I said. "We'll talk more about it when I come back."

The three of us had lunch, and then I went into the other room and changed into the MVD uniform.

By the time I reached the Hall of Columns, the trial was already underway—which was what I wanted. The corridor was empty except for the glass-covered case and the solitary guard. I entered the building from the other side and walked down the corridor to the front. This time no one paid any attention to me as I passed the offices, I was only another uniform.

The guard at the case looked up in curiosity as I approached. "What is this?" he asked. "Am I being relieved early?"

"For a few minutes," I said. "I will stay here until you return—if you do."

"What do you mean by that?"

I shrugged. "Perhaps they will give you another assignment. All I know is that I was called into the office and ordered to come here. You are to report there at once to Colonel Sergeiev."

"Who the devil is Colonel Sergeiev?" he demanded.

"From the Komitet Gosudarstvennoy Bezopasnosti," I said.

He paled at the mention of the KGB. "What do they want to talk to me about?"

"How should I know?" I retorted. "Do you see any decorations on my uniform that they should take me into their confidence? I only follow orders as you do. And yours are to go at once to the office and see Colonel Sergeiev. I will guard the spy's things. Although I do not think he will be trying to get them back."

"That is true," he said, but his mind was on other things. "Well, I suppose I should be going ..."

"I think so," I agreed solemnly.

He started off with a worried look on his face, then looked back. "What is your name, Comrade?"

"Chernicov," I said. "Good luck, Comrade."

He nodded absent-mindedly and walked on. I watched impatiently for him to disappear around the bend in the corridor. Then I would have two minutes, three at the very most, before he discovered there was no Colonel Sergeiev, no Chernicov, and no orders for him to report at the office. And within one minute after that there would be several men pounding down the corridor looking for me.

He moved out of sight. There was no time for niceties such as picking the lock. I lifted my gun and smashed the butt down on the glass. It broke with a crash. I reached through the jagged spears of glass and grabbed the map. I moved swiftly toward the front entrance, stuffing it into my pocket. Even as I went through the door, I thought I heard a shout somewhere back in the corridor.

I went down the steps to the street level and looked around. Immediately in front of the hall a number Zim limousines were parked with no one in them. Farther down to the left a Pobeda, something like a small Chevrolet, was parked in front of a tobacco store. A man was sitting behind the wheel. I turned and strode quickly down to it.

"Move this car out of here," I ordered, "and make it fast."

"But I'm waiting for someone in there," he said, gesturing toward the Hall of Columns.

"I don't care who you're waiting for," I snapped. "Khrushchev is arriving here any minute, and the street is to be cleared. Drive out of here as fast as you can—or I may take you off the street myself."

He looked startled, but he obeyed. He started the car and pulled away, gunning the motor as much as he could. I turned and stepped into the tobacco shop. And none too soon. As I stood at the counter, I saw seven or eight men come running out of the Hall of Columns. They stopped to look around and caught sight of the Pobeda speeding away. They all piled into a Zim and gave chase as soon as they could get it started.

I bought a package of cigarettes, walked down to the first block, and turned left. Another block away, I caught a bus. I rode it for about fifteen blocks and got off. I caught another bus going the opposite way and stayed on for five blocks. Then I took a taxi.

Yuri was already with Ilya and Natasha when I reached the apartment. They all three looked relieved as I came in.

"You got it?" Natasha asked excitedly as she closed the door.

"Yes," I said. I took the map from my pocket and went immediately to the stove. I took a dish from the cupboard above and then held a match to the map.

"Give me another minute," I told them. I went into the other room and changed back to my own clothes. I returned to them carrying the uniform.

"This must be destroyed as quickly as possible," I said.

"There is an incinerator in the building," Natasha said. "Just down the hall. I'll put it in there."

"Good girl," I said, handing the uniform to her. She took it and hurried out the door. She was back within a couple of minutes.

"The gun may still be a risk," I said, "but I'm going to need it, so I'll take that one. I think I got away all right, but they're going to start a big hunt, and I think I may have made one mistake." I told them about the taxi I'd taken, and they confirmed my guess. MVD men usually did not pay when they wanted to ride in cabs.

"But it may be all right," Yuri said. "The driver may be so pleased at getting paid that he will keep his mouth shut. And you did leave the taxi three blocks away."

"Maybe," I said. "But once he hears about the search for a phony MVD man, he may be frightened enough to report it. But the time it will take for that to happen may be long enough. What about the car, Yuri?"

"It is there," he said. "To take it will be easy."

"And the clothes?" I asked Natasha.

"In the other room. I should have told you so you wouldn't have to change twice."

"It's all right," I said. "I have a little time. Ilya, describe the streets on that route again."

"Yuri knows them even better than I do," he said.

We brought out the diagram that Ilya had made, and Yuri looked at it. He then gave me a minute, almost photographic description of the route of the car as it would take Cooper back to the prison. I finally settled on what looked like the best place, the last six blocks before the prison. From Yuri's description, it sounded narrow enough for what I had in mind. Yuri had said that two cars could barely pass. I put my finger on what looked to be about halfway along that stretch.

"What is along here, Yuri?" I asked.

"Workers' apartments," he said. "Perhaps one or two small stores. That is all."

"Are the people who live there apt to interfere?"

"If they see uniformed men fighting with another man, they'll lock the doors and pull the blinds down. They know that in such a case it is better to be completely ignorant."

"In this case, I approve," I said. "Well, we'll leave in about an hour and a half." I went into the other room and got the gun. I wanted to check it over thoroughly and be sure that everything was in perfect working order before I started.

"You will shoot the three guards?" Yuri asked eagerly.

"I don't know," I confessed. "I hope I don't have to shoot, but I may not be able to avoid it. I'll have to see how it works out."

I think Yuri looked disappointed, but we turned to other details. Natasha had checked and verified that the girl upstairs was still on her vacation. I would bring Cooper back to this apartment, then go up and pick the lock and move him there. Yuri had looked into airfields not too far from Moscow and thought he'd found a small one that had possibilities. He was going to try to find out more. Ilya suggested that the best way of getting to the airfield would be to buy a small car on the black market and drive as near there as possible. He thought that mere boldness might get us through, especially if we used a popular small car that many families used for their vacations. All the suggestions sounded possible, and we still had some time to decide on the best.

I changed into the old clothes, and transferred my papers and other possessions. Then Yuri and I left. We took a bus, transferred to another one, and finally ended up in a section of Moscow I had never seen before. We walked three blocks after getting off the second bus. Yuri finally stopped on a street corner and pointed in the direction we were facing.

"There it is," he said proudly.

There was only one car parked on the street, so there was no chance of making a mistake. Yuri had certainly followed my instructions to the letter. I had never seen an older or shabbier car. It evidently dated from the time when the Russians were copying our Fords, and it looked as if they had also copied the idea of repairing it with baling wire.

"Are you sure it will run?" I asked.

"Oh, it runs very good," Yuri said. 'You want me to go show you?"

"I'll steal my own cars, Yuri," I said. "Where is the owner?"

"On the next block. Drinking vodka. He will be there for two hours or more. Nobody else will pay any attention. They hate him. So much that if the car doesn't start at once, they may rush out and give you a push."

"Now, how do I get to Nevka Street?"

His face lit up. "You see, I told you that you need me. The way is very complicated, but I will show you."

"All right," I said, giving in. "But as soon as we're near the place, you'll have to get out."

He grinned, and we started down the street. We reached the car and climbed in. I hadn't really believed Yuri, but certainly no one made an outcry or paid any attention to us. I reached under the instrument panel, disconnected the ignition wires, and wired them together. I stepped on the starter. I don't think I expected anything to happen, but the motor started at once. It didn't sound too bad. I put it in gear and we moved off.

We reached a spot near my destination without mishap. I stopped the car and told Yuri to get out. He put up a little argument, but finally did.

"I'll see you back at the apartment," I told him, and drove off. I had a few minutes to spare and drove slowly. I finally reached the spot about fifteen minutes before the car with Cooper was due to arrive there. Yuri had described the street perfectly. By turning and backing I finally got the car directly across the street. There was no room for another car to get by on either side. I killed the motor and got out.

I went around to the front and lifted the hood. Then I reached down and ripped the wires from the carburetor. While I was at it, I got some grease, and smeared it around on my hands and a little on my face. I put the hood down and went back to sit behind the wheel. I waited until I knew the car was about due, then began stepping on the starter.

I was aware when the car arrived, but I didn't look up. The starter whirred with a dismal sound. The horn blew on the other car. I looked up, waved hopelessly at the car, and continued to press the starter.

The driver leaned out of the window. "Get out of the way," he ordered.

"I can't," I said. "It will not start."

"Then push it out of the way," he said.

I shrugged, and gave up with the starter. I made sure the hand brake was partly set, and climbed out. I got behind the car and pushed, but nothing happened. I saw the men in the car exchanging words, then the driver got out and came over to me.

"Come on," he said roughly. "We have to get this junk pile out of the street. We are on government business."

I gave him a sickly smile and gestured futilely at the car again. He muttered under his breath but put his own shoulder against it. We both pushed, but I didn't work too hard and the car still didn't move. We struggled for a couple of minutes and finally the driver straightened up, looked at the other car, and shrugged. There was some more conversation there, while I held my breath, then the rear door of the car opened and one of the KGB men got out. He left the door open. Inside I could see the other guard and Cooper.

The KGB man came over and scowled at me. "This time we'd better get this car out of the way or we will arrest you. Understand?"

"Yes, sir," I said.

One of them got on either side of me and put his shoulder to the car. I did the same, facing the one who had his back to me. As I pushed, I reached for my gun.

The car began to move slowly despite the brakes. I straightened up, and turned to face the man back of me. The gun barrel raked across his forehead before he even knew what was happening. Without waiting to see him fall, I whirled on the other one. He had already guessed that something had happened, and he was trying to turn and get his gun out at the same time. But he was at a disadvantage. He was off balance, and his back was toward me. Before he could make it, I brought the gun down on his head. He grunted and collapsed.

Two down, I muttered to myself, and looked at the car. The other KGB man had his gun out and was lining it up on me. I dropped to the ground behind the MVD man. The other gun went off, and I heard the bullet over my head. By then I had him in my sights. I pulled the trigger gently, and saw him slump back against the seat. His gun dropped out of the car.

I jumped to my feet and ran over. The guard wasn't dead, or even unconscious. He was leaning against the back of the seat, one hand clutching his shoulder, the blood coming out be tween his fingers. He glared at me and tensed his body.

"Don't try it," I told him in Russian. "I can't miss you this close."

He struggled with himself and lost the battle. He stayed where he was, watching me closely. I turned my attention to Cooper. He was sitting there, looking as if he didn't believe what he saw.

"What is this?" he said as though he didn't expect an answer.

"It's what they used to call the arrival of the U.S. Cavalry," I told him in English. "A modern version of an old-fashioned rescue. Come on, Cooper, let's get out of here, *fast!*"

"I don't believe it," he said. "You read stuff like this in books, but it doesn't happen. I'm only a sky jockey. Nobody is going to send the Cavalry to rescue me."

"Somebody did," I said impatiently. "Come on, we don't have all day. This place will be swarming with cops any minute."

He was shaking his head. "It was mighty nice of you to make the effort, *but I'm not going with you!*"

I had expected almost anything but this. "What?" I asked.

"I'm not going with you," he repeated.

"Why in the hell not?" I demanded.

"My dad and two brothers are landing here tonight," he said slowly. "What do you think would happen to them if I escaped?"

"They wouldn't dare do anything to them," I said.

He was shaking his head again. "I ain't going to risk it. My lawyer says I won't get more than seven years. I can do that and still find my family alive when I get home."

I looked at him with speculation.

"You can't do it," he said, guessing what I was thinking. "If you try to knock me out and drag me, you'll never make it. ... You may not anyway unless you leave at once."

He was right. I knew it, but I hated to be cheated after everything that had been done. But I didn't have any time. I kicked the guard's gun under the car and looked at the other two guards. They were still out. I turned and ran.

"Give my regards to the Statue of Liberty when you see her," Cooper called after me.

I didn't bother to answer. I knew I was going to have my hands full for the next few minutes, at least until I could get back to the apartment and change clothes. I ran swiftly for two zigzag blocks, then slowed down to a fast walk. I threw the gun away. I wanted to keep it, but it would be too damning as evidence if it was found. Two more blocks away, I saw a small car parked with no one around it. I slipped into it, tore out the ignition wires, and put them together. Then I drove away. As I left the curb I heard a shout behind me but ignored it.

I left the car at the curb a good ten blocks away from the apartment house, and went the rest of the way on foot, keeping a sharp eye out for cops. I was about two blocks away from the apartment when I suddenly saw Natasha on the street ahead of me. At the same time she saw me, and started for me as fast as she could walk. Her face was white with tension and I knew something had happened.

"What's wrong?"

"We can't stand here. We must walk away from here." She led the way along the first cross street. "They arrested Ilya and Yuri. A half hour ago."

"Who?"

"KGB, I think. I was out and came back just in time to see them being led out into the streets."

"Do you know why?"

"No. One never knows. We may have been on a suspicion list, or someone may have made a report about us. Anything. And there are still guards on the apartment. Did you leave your papers there?"

"No."

"Then you can get away. That's why I waited on the street. I hoped I would see you before they found me."

"They won't find you now," I said.

"They will," she said. "No one can live in Russia without papers, and now I have no papers I can use."

"We'll find a way," I said. "But first we've got to hole up somewhere. There's probably already a description of me around. Do you know of a hotel where they don't frown on a girl visiting a man in his room?"

"The Molenka, I think. I believe I heard Yuri talking about it once."

"All right. First, let's go somewhere where I can buy clothes."

We took the subway, getting off at a stop Natasha knew. She led the way to a small clothing store and I succeeded in buying a suit that wasn't too bad. I bought a few other things and some clothes for her. There was no place for me to change there, but we went back to the subway and I changed in the men's room. I stuffed the old clothes under some paper in a trash basket and we went on to the hotel.

She was right about the hotel. The clerk looked at my papers and I signed the register. I explained that the girl wasn't staying long, and for a minute I thought he was going to wink at me.

"We'll be safe here for a while," I told her when we were in the room, "but we'd better not stay too long. The hunt for me will probably be overshadowed by the one for you, but there's always a chance someone will want to see your papers. And in the hunt for me, they may eventually get down to checking all the guests in hotels. I'll be all right until they make a call to Rostov. So we'd better put our minds to getting out of Moscow."

"How can I get out?" she asked. "And where would I go if I did get out?"

"To America, with me," I said.

"America?"

"Why not? You're a member of the Russian underground, and you should be very welcome. You'll probably get a job right away. You could be valuable."

"You think so?" she exclaimed. Then her face fell. "It is awful to think that I might get out just when Ilya and Yuri have been caught."

"I don't think we can do anything about that," I said gently. "If I hadn't created such an uproar, I might have been able to—but not now. We'll have to go, Natasha. I'm sure that Ilya and Yuri would agree."

Then she came into my arms and cried until she was exhausted.

We stayed in the hotel for two days, while I thought up ways of escaping and discarded them. The search was too big for either a black market car or another stolen one. The papers were full of the story of the American agent who had tried to rescue Cooper, and it had even started Khrushchev off on another tirade of threats against America. In the meantime, everyone there had denied knowing anything about an agent.

Finally I hit on an idea I thought might work. Leaving Natasha in the hotel room, I spent two nights down at the trucking center in Moscow. Most of it was spent in little cafés, drinking vodka and listening to the truck drivers.

The third night we both went down. By this time I was familiar with which trucks were which. Standing in the shadows, we watched a big six-wheeler being loaded for Leningrad. When it was loaded, the two drivers went into the café for a last drink. We slipped out of our shadow and quickly climbed in the back. We made ourselves as comfortable as we could on the boxes, and a few minutes later we were on our way.

All through the night the big truck roared along, and well into the next day. I had been watching the time, and when it seemed we should be nearing Leningrad, I slipped to the rear and began to watch through the tarpaulin. When we finally reached Leningrad, we looked for our chance, and as the truck went around a sharp corner, we dropped off.

In Leningrad we took a trolley to the center of the city, and I found a bus terminal. I bought two tickets to Tallinn, south of Leningrad, getting them one at a time and from different windows just in case someone wanted to see papers. But nothing happened and we were soon on the bus heading south.

Tallinn was a little more of a problem. We were there two days and nights and getting a little nervous, before I found a fisherman I could bribe to take us across the narrow neck of the Baltic to Finland. It wasn't the most ideal place to go, but I had little choice. That night the fisherman took us, and a couple of hours later we were at the American Embassy.

It took a little more doing to get them to awaken the Ambassador, but it was finally accomplished, and a handsome, gray-haired man in a fancy bathrobe was peering at us curiously.

"I'm a major in the United States Army," I told him. "For security reasons, I can't tell you any more than that at the moment. I want to make a phone call to General Sam Roberts, in Washington."

He must have heard of the General, but he didn't even blink. "That's a most unusual request, Major. Would you mind if the call was made in my presence?"

"No, sir."

"Then come on," he said. He led the way to his office and indicated the phone. I picked it up and put in the call. It took a while for it to get through, but finally there was General Roberts on the other end.

"General," I said, "this is your favorite chestnut puller. Have you been keeping up with your reading?"

"I'll say I have," he said. "We were worried about you, boy. I see where things didn't go quite right. How bad is it?"

"Not too bad. The first problem went off fine; the second didn't because the prize pupil didn't want to play."

He whistled. "Where are you now?"

"The American Embassy in Finland. And I'm homesick. Incidentally, you remember the three friends I was to look up?"

"Yes."

"One of them is with me. The young lady. The other two were unable to make it."

"I see," he said. He was silent for a minute. "I guess maybe the best way is the simplest. Less possible complications. Tell the Ambassador to expect a call from the State Department. We'll see you soon. Got any money left?"

"Enough to get back on."

"Okay, boy. Goodbye."

He hung up, and I told the Ambassador about the expected call. He had some brandy brought in, and we all sat and waited together. The call came in a half hour. I don't know what he was told, but it seemed to cheer him up. "Well, Major," he said, slapping me on the back when he'd finished, "why didn't you just tell me your troubles? No problem at all. We find a couple of rooms for you and the young lady, and everything will be fixed up in the morning."

I didn't know what he meant by that, but I kept my mouth shut. And I found out in the morning. Right after breakfast, we were handed two passports good for passage one way from Finland to America. The names on them weren't ours, but obviously the Ambassador didn't know that.

"Anybody can lose his passport, Major Johnson," he said. "No need to call Washington about that."

"I'm the cautious type," I said, and let it go at that.

That afternoon Natasha and I boarded a regular jetliner for America. When we'd unbuckled our seatbelts and leaned back, I lit a cigarette. "Well, honey," I said, "you'll soon be in America."

"I know," she said. She sounded excited. "Will I see you again after we are there?"

"Definitely."

"It will be wonderful. Still … I think I may miss Moscow in the spring."

"And the red, red flowers?" I asked, quoting from the password I had used when I first met her. "Well, there will still be flowers blooming there, and maybe one day the whole country will bloom."

She smiled and put her head on my shoulder. A few minutes later she was asleep.

6

The Twisted Trap

The Intercontinental Insurance Company will insure you against almost anything, including snow on the Fourth of July, but they've never gotten around to issuing a policy to cover a guy flipping his wig. That's why I wasn't too interested when I first saw Herbert J. Wolfe.

The name is March. Milo March. I'm an insurance investigator. With my own office on Madison Avenue, the buckle on the Martini Belt in New York City. I'm at the beck and call of any insurance company that can afford to pay a hundred dollars a day and expenses.

I was in between cases, and things were slow that morning. I was sitting in my office and working on a case. Well, it wasn't exactly a case, just one bottle of V.O. I kept it in the filing cabinet, under R for relaxation. Then the phone rang. I picked up the receiver and said hello.

"Milo, boy, how are you?" a man's voice asked. I recognized it. Martin Raymond, vice-president of Intercontinental Insurance, one of the companies that could afford the fees I charge.

"Hello, Martin," I said. "I was wondering when you were going to call and ask me how I was feeling."

"You know how it is," he said. I didn't, but I wasn't going to argue with him. "Do you have any free time, Milo?"

"I have some time, but it isn't free."

"We should know," he said, trying to sound like one of the boys. "I'd like you to run up here for a minute, if you will. We'll pay you, of course."

"Of course," I said. "What's the problem?"

"I don't know," he admitted. "A Mr. Wolfe, one of our policyholders, just came in and says he wants to save the company five hundred thousand dollars, but he won't talk to anyone except an investigator."

"Did he say how he's going to save the company that much?"

"No. He's probably a crackpot, but we do carry a policy on him for two hundred and fifty thousand dollars. Double indemnity in case of accidental death."

"Which adds up to five hundred thousand," I observed. "All right. I'll be there as soon as I can."

I hung up and took a last fond drink from the bottle before I put it away in the filing cabinet. I went downstairs and got a cab. The Intercontinental Building was only ten blocks up Madison Avenue and we were soon there. I went upstairs and entered into the reception room, a plush place presided over by a receptionist who was a tasty little number—if you were mathematically minded.

"Oh, Mr. March," she said as I came in, "Mr. Raymond said to tell you that a man is waiting for you in the conference room and you're to go there directly. Shall I show you?"

"You already have," I said. Which was true. Every time she

bent over her desk to speak to someone it was an education in the difference between men and women.

"Oh, you!" she exclaimed. She was an Einstein in the body department only.

I went through a door to the left and walked down to the conference room. It was a quietly luxurious room, with a table about the size of a tennis court and a number of chairs that were supposed to make the room look like Buckingham Palace. There was a man in one of the chairs. He was a short, slender man who looked to be about sixty. He was wearing an expensive brown suit, rumpled as though he'd taken a nap in it. His hair was thinning on top, but what was left of it was gray. I thought he looked timid enough to leap out of the chair if I made a sudden move.

"Hello," I said. "I'm Milo March, an investigator for Intercontinental. You're Mr. ... Wolfe?"

"Herbert J. Wolfe," he said. He was perched on the edge of the chair as though waiting for the starting gun. "I'm glad you're here, Mr. March. I don't have much time. They'll probably be after me any minute."

"They?" I asked.

He nodded. "I think they may have seen me come into this building. A phone call to my wife would make it very simple to deduce which floor I'm visiting. That's why I'd better get right to the point about the policy."

I was beginning to have my suspicions about Herbert. "You did mention something about saving the company money," I murmured.

"Precisely," he said. "I have a policy with your company

for two hundred and fifty thousand dollars. It was taken out three years ago. The sole beneficiary is my wife, Nancy. The policy pays five hundred thousand in the event of accidental death. I presume that you would prefer not paying the face value at this moment, and I assure you that I would prefer that you didn't have to pay it. That's why I'm here."

"I see," I said, which is what you always say when you don't see.

"Do you really?" he asked eagerly. "Splendid. Then I won't have to waste time repeating myself. You see, it's very simple. About six months ago my wife, who is considerably younger than myself, got me to see a new doctor. A Dr. Howard Borden. He's a psychiatrist as well as a physician. He examined me and recommended some medicine. For my nerves, he said. Bosh! I never had a nerve in my life. Anyway, I began having spells shortly after I started taking the medicine."

"Spells?" I asked. I didn't think it was leading anywhere, but at least I'd get a hundred dollars for the day.

"Yes," he said. "Bad ones. When they first started, I thought I was losing my mind. It's only recently that I realized what was causing them."

"What?"

"I believe I mentioned that my wife is younger than I am," he said. "In fact, she's almost forty years younger. Dr. Borden is a fairly young man. I have reason to believe they are interested in each other. I started having the spells after Dr. Borden prescribed medicine for me. He gave me a second medicine, which did help the spells, but insisted on my still taking the first medicine. Then two weeks ago he and my wife prevailed upon me to go to his sanatorium on Long Island. I was supposed to go for observation for only two or three days. Once I was there the spells became more frequent and he has not let me leave. I have been virtually a prisoner until this morning, when I managed to escape. But they are after me and I'm sure they will find me here."

What do you say to a guy with a story like that? "Well … it's an interesting story, Mr. Wolfe, but I'm not quite sure why you came here with it. Why not go to the police?"

He shook his head. "I have no proof. Since I've been in the sanatorium I don't even have the medicine in my possession. Dr. Borden's word, under the circumstances, might be enough to have me legally committed. But I assure you, Mr. March, I'm not insane."

"Of course not," I said hastily. "But I still think the police are your best bet, Mr. Wolfe."

"They wouldn't believe me." He hunched forward in his chair. "Mr. March, I'm convinced that my wife and Dr. Borden intend to continue this treatment until they can have me declared legally insane. Then there will be some sort of accident in which I will be killed and my wife will collect a half million dollars from your company. Wouldn't you like to keep that from happening?"

"I don't know how—" I started to explain. I was interrupted by the phone ringing. I went over and picked up the receiver and answered it.

"I'm sorry, Mr. March," the receptionist said, "but there are two men here who say that they are from a sanatorium and they've come for that Mr. Wolfe who's with you. They say he escaped from the sanatorium."

"I know," I told her. "I guess you might as well let them come on back." I put the receiver down and made myself look at him.

"They're here?" he asked quietly.

I nodded. "I'm sorry, Mr. Wolfe, but there really isn't anything I can do. You did escape from the sanatorium, and if I tried to keep them out they could have me arrested. There is no evidence of any crime, and I can't interfere even though you are insured by this company."

"I understand," he said. "I guess it was just a desperate hope." He stood up and half turned to face the door, waiting. "Thank you for your time, Mr. March."

Before I could answer they knocked on the door. It was a heavy knock, as if whoever was doing it didn't care whether he knocked the door down or not.

"Come in," I said.

The door swung open and they came in. Two of them. They were big, both well over six feet and close to two hundred pounds each. They looked like pugs, their faces craggy and scarred.

"There he is," one of them said. They moved in on either side of the old man and grabbed him roughly.

"Take it easy," I said.

The bigger one of the two looked at me. "Keep out of this, buster. It's none of your business."

I didn't like his tone. "Maybe I'll buy in," I said evenly. "It looks like a cheap business."

He took a longer look at me. He wasn't any friendlier, but

he must have realized he was showing too much muscle. His face moved in what was supposed to be a smile. "Sorry to bust in like this," he said, "but the old boy escaped from the sanatorium this morning. I'm the head guard there. Name's Hardin. It's Dr. Borden's sanatorium on Long Island if you want to check with the doc."

"I know all about that," I said. "I was merely saying that you didn't have to be so rough with Mr. Wolfe."

"Sure," he said, but I couldn't see that his grip eased up any. "Say, what'd he want to see you for?"

I looked at the old man and for the first time realized that it was fear I saw in his eyes, not timidity. I still should have kept out of it, but before I fully realized what was happening I had opened my big mouth. "Mr. Wolfe," I said, "came in to discuss the possibility of taking out more insurance."

Then I was glad that I had said it, for there was a look of gratitude on the old man's face.

"Yeah?" the guard said. "Shows how batty he is. Well, thanks for keeping him here until we caught up. Come on, Mr. Wolfe, we're going to take you back to the nursery."

They pushed the old man ahead of them through the door. The last I saw of him, he was looking back at me and the fear was still in his eyes.

I stayed in the conference room for a few minutes, trying to think about what had happened, but all I could see was the look in the old man's eyes. Finally I went in to see Raymond. I gave him a quick outline of what had happened and waited.

"Sounds like he flipped his wig," he said uncertainly. "Maybe we can cancel the policy ..."

"You know better than that," I said. "You wouldn't have a chance. And maybe Wolfe has flipped and is writing the script himself. On the other hand, maybe not. You want to save the company five hundred thousand pieces of the long green?"

He looked as if I'd just asked him if he wanted a reserve seat in Heaven. "Naturally we want to protect the Intercontinental stockholders as much as possible. What did you have in mind?"

"I thought I might check up on the story. If it looks as if he's off his rocker, I'll drop it. If not, I'll see what I can dig up that'll stop it."

"It's a delicate situation," he said. "Actually, we have no right to interfere until a claim is made."

"On the other hand, there is a half million dollars," I said.

He nodded. He'd been thinking about that all along. "I suppose we do have a moral responsibility to policyholders," he said. He cleared his throat. "I suppose you should see what you can find out, Milo. Of course, in a case like this, if anything should go wrong I don't see how we can back you up."

"Meaning I'll be on my own and you won't admit that you even hired me?" I knew damn well that was what he meant.

"Something like that."

"Okay," I said cheerfully. I stood up and started to back out of the office.

"What the devil are you doing?" he asked irritably.

"Just being careful not to turn my back on you," I said sweetly. I was gone before he could think of an answer.

ILLUSTRATED BY HARVEY KIDDER

I went into another part of the offices and got the file on Herbert Wolfe. He had taken out the policy three years earlier, shortly before he was married. His wife was the sole benefi- ciary. He'd been fifty-eight when they were married and his wife was twenty-one. She'd been in the chorus of a Broadway musical. The policy investigator had recorded the fact that she was a tasty dish and he hadn't been under any illusion that the marriage was a great love match, but he also hadn't found anything to indicate that the bride had homicidal tendencies. His report indicated he thought she was willing for time to take care of the matter. Herbert Wolfe was worth somewhere in the neighborhood of a million dollars—and that's a nice section to live in. But the investigation showed that most of his estate would go to three children by an earlier marriage, which seemed to explain the reason for the large policy with the new wife as beneficiary.

I made a note of the address and put the folder back. Then I went on uptown to a modest little shack of five stories between Madison and Park Avenues. I rang the bell and after a while a little black-haired maid came to the door.

"Mrs. Wolfe," I said. "My name is March and I'm from her husband's insurance company."

"I will see," she said doubtfully. She left me outside and went off to do her seeing.

It didn't take her long. She came back and opened the door. "Mrs. Wolfe will see you for a moment," she said. "I will show you."

She led the way up the stairs and I followed. She was wearing a tight-fitting black uniform and the view was fine. I didn't care how many flights of stairs we had to climb. I wondered about Mrs. Wolfe; a woman would have to feel pretty sure about herself to have competition like that around the house.

Then I found out about Mrs. Wolfe. We reached the second floor and the maid led me into a room. "Mr. March," she murmured, and slipped back past me.

She'd been sitting in a large chair but she stood up as I entered the room. The Intercontinental investigator had certainly understated the case. She had golden blond hair down to her shoulders, framing a beautiful face highlighted by the sultriest pair of lips I'd ever seen. She wore a red dress that had been fitted so as to put the least possible strain on anyone's imagination.

"Mr. March?" she asked. There was a little smile tugging at her lips as though she knew what was running through my mind.

"That's right," I said. I let my gaze have another holiday running over her figure again. "You are Mrs. Wolfe?"

"Yes."

"No wonder your husband is anxious to come home."

She laughed, but some of her poise was gone. "And this," she said, "is Dr. Howard Borden. Herbert's doctor—and mine."

I hadn't noticed him before, but then he wasn't as fancy as she was. He'd been in the background, but now he stepped forward with his hand out and a professional smile on his face. I looked him over carefully before taking his hand. He was a good-looking man, maybe about thirty-five or forty. There was really nothing wrong with him, but I disliked him at first glance. He was too handsome, too well dressed in his Brooks Brothers suit, a little too smooth—but with a hardness beneath the smooth exterior.

"Dr. Borden came in this morning as soon as he discovered Herbert was missing," the blonde was saying. "He knew that I would be terribly upset, and then we both thought that Herbert might come here."

"That was kind of him," I said as I shook hands with the doctor.

"Professional kindness," he said with a deprecating smile. "Fortunately my men saw him when he went to his bank. They trailed him to your building, then called here. It was very kind of you, Mr. March, to keep him occupied until my men reached you."

"Professional kindness," I said, matching his smile. "Tell me, Dr. Borden, what kind of doctor are you?"

"Medical doctor and analyst." There was a little more starch in his tone.

"And you have a sanatorium on Long Island?"

"Yes. For those of my patients who are more severely disturbed and can afford private care."

"Where is it?"

"Laurelton."

"And is Mr. Wolfe one of your more severely disturbed patients?"

"Mr. March," the blonde said, "I don't understand this. Why are you here and why are you asking all these questions?"

"Your husband," I said, "told me he wants to take out another insurance policy for the same amount as the one he has. With you as beneficiary. Since he is in a sanatorium, we want to know something about his condition before we consider it."

That was nice bait I was throwing out, and if the old man was right, it might save his life for a few extra days.

"That's different," the blonde said. "I didn't know Herbert

had anything like that in mind. How sweet of him to think of me when he's so ill."

"Yes," the doctor said smoothly. "It does change the picture. To answer your question, Mr. March, Mr. Wolfe is badly disturbed."

"In what way?"

"Schizophrenia."

I made a face. "Sounds serious. Is it?"

"Very serious, but not in a way that should bother your company. As long as he is watched and cared for, Mr. Wolfe should live out his normal life span. I even have high hopes of curing him. We have made many advances in treating this type of mental illness."

"How long has he been ill?"

"I detected the first symptoms about six months ago and started treating him at once."

"I see," I said. I looked at the blonde. "How did you happen to call Dr. Borden? Were you in analysis with him?"

"I went to him a year ago when I was having trouble sleeping. I thought I might need analysis, but he said I didn't. When I first noticed Herbert acting strangely, I immediately thought of Dr. Borden."

"Naturally," I said. "Well, I guess that's all for now. We'll let Mr. Wolfe know what we decide. It will be all right to phone him at the sanatorium, won't it?"

"Of course," the doctor said promptly. "He may not always be able to come to the phone, you understand. There are times when he is not very rational."

"I understand," I said. I thanked both of them, the doctor

shook my hand, and the blonde gave me a smile that almost had me hanging on the ropes. As soon as I could get my breath again, I left.

I thought about them on the way back to the office. They had made everything sound all right: poor old Herbert was off his rocker and they were doing the best they could for him. It was very touching, but I didn't like it. For one thing there'd been a faint smear of red on the good doctor's collar. It had been the same color and shade as the blonde's lipstick. Or maybe that was my dirty mind at work.

I went back to Intercontinental and went in to see Dr. Evans, the head of their medical department.

"What's up?" he asked as I came in. "I don't usually see you unless someone has pulled a fast one. I haven't heard of any contested claim."

"I think I'm trying to prevent one being made," I said. "You know anything about schizophrenia?"

"A little," he grunted. "Why? Think you've got it?"

"Stick to medical jokes," I told him. "Let's do a little supposing. Suppose I wanted to commit a man to a mental institution, only there's nothing wrong with him. Could I give him schizophrenia, or at least make him and others think he had it?"

He sat up a little straighter in his chair. "You couldn't give it to him, but there is a way you could give him the worst symptoms so that even a doctor might be fooled. But it would be difficult for you to get the particular drug."

"Even if I were a medical doctor and an analyst with my own private sanatorium?"

"No, then it wouldn't. There's a drug known as lysergic acid diethylamide. A small amount of it will make a healthy man have every symptom of advanced schizophrenia. After several hours, the symptoms will pass and the man will be normal again. It's been used by a number of doctors who have taken it themselves in order to learn more about the experiences of the schizophrenic."

"Is there anything that will serve as an antidote?"

"Well, yes. Chlorpromazine will bring one out of it pretty quickly."*

"Let's suppose something else," I said. "Say once I've established that he's schizophrenic, I want to kill him. Can't I arrange for him to escape from the sanatorium, then shove him in front of a car or something of the sort and nobody will question it?"

"I suppose so," the doctor said slowly. "You could also kill him with electric shocks. Electric shock therapy is often used with schizophrenics, and sometimes there is a mistake. Are you going to tell me what this is all about?"

"Not now. Maybe later, if it works out."

"This mythical patient of yours," he said. "Does he have a policy with Intercontinental?"

"A big one."

"Well, you can double-check if you want to. If it's a big policy, you can be sure we have the man's complete medi-

---

* In *The Splintered Man,* which has a similar plot element, an Author's Note states: "Everything said about lysergic acid diethylamide (LSD) is as accurate as I could make it. I have taken certain liberties with chlorpromazine in extrapolating the uses to which it may still be put." The antipsychotic drug chlorpromazine, also known by the trade names Thorazine and Largactil, is not a true antidote that would instantly reverse the effects of LSD in the way portrayed in the book and story.

cal history. If he's a schizophrenic, there ought to be some evidence of it. How old is he?"

"Sixty-one."

"Schizophrenia is a condition that hits you young, usually before twenty," he said. "So there should be some evidence of it in his medical record."

"I've looked at it," I told him. "This policyholder was as healthy as a horse all his life. Well, thanks, Doc. I'll send you bulletins from the bedside."

I left the insurance building. I stopped off for some lunch, then went back to my office. Once I tried calling Herbert Wolfe at the sanatorium. I got Dr. Borden, who said that Herbert was having one of his spells. He offered to take a message, but I said I'd call back the next day. I went back to sitting and thinking. Finally I made a decision.

Before I left the office, I checked to see who I knew on the Nassau County police force. It turned out to be a lieutenant. I called him and asked him to have one of his squad cars keep an eye on Borden's Sanatorium that night. He didn't like it because I refused to give him a reason, but he finally agreed. Then I left the office and went back to the insurance company to see Dr. Evans. It took a little talking, but I finally got him to give me a prescription for enough chlorpromazine to offset one dose of lysergic acid. I had the prescription filled, took the pills out of the box, and put them in my pocket.

I had dinner in town, killed a little more time at the bar, and finally caught a train for Laurelton. It was about ten o'clock when I got there.

I had already looked up the location of the sanatorium on

a map. It was about a half mile from the station. I decided to walk instead of taking a cab.

The sanatorium was a huge, sprawling building that must have once been the mansion of the neighborhood. It was surrounded by a high stone wall. There were lights in the house, but the grounds were dark. I went around to the back. I jumped, caught the top of the wall, and managed to pull myself up. It was a little too athletic for my taste, but it seemed to be the only way in except through the front gates. I dropped down on the inside, hoping the doctor didn't keep dogs. I hadn't thought of it before or I might have brought a steak. I headed for the back of the house.

I had almost reached the house and was just beginning to congratulate myself on my cleverness when something happened. A small, hard object was shoved into the middle of my back.

"Okay, buster," a voice said. "Just keep on marching careful-like into the house and you won't get hurt—yet."

I recognized the voice. It belonged to the guard who had been in the office to get Herbert Wolfe. I also recognized the object against my back. It was a gun, so I marched.

"Open the door," he said when we reached the house, "and step inside real slow and careful. Don't try any tricks."

I opened the door and stepped inside. He followed me.

"Now let's see who you are," he said. He grabbed my shoulder and swung me around. He grinned when he saw my face. "Well, if it ain't the guy who thought I was too rough this morning. The Doc is going to want to see you." Holding the gun against me, he ran one hand over my body, but I hadn't brought a gun with me. He straightened up and nudged me with his gun. "Let's go, buster." I went. There wasn't anything else to do.

We reached the front of the house and he ordered me to stop in front of a closed door. He told me to knock on the door. I did.

"Come in," a voice called from the room. It was Dr. Borden's voice.

"Open the door and walk in," the guard said.

I did as he told me. I was in what seemed to be a combination office and study. Dr. Borden was sitting behind a desk, going through some papers. He looked up and for a moment there was surprise on his face as he recognized me.

"Look what I caught," the guard said from behind me. "I saw him come over the wall and start sneaking up on the house, so I decided to invite him in. He's that insurance fellow the old guy went to see."

"I know," Dr. Borden said. "I've met Mr. March. Good work, Jack. Is he armed?"

"No. I guess it's a friendly visit."

"Okay, but stay and watch him." The doctor's gaze came back to me. "What are you doing here, March?"

"I've joined the Gray Ladies,"* I said. "I was coming to visit Mr. Wolfe."

"Why didn't you try the front gate?"

"I'm the modest type," I said. "I never feel right unless I come in the back way."

---

* The Gray Ladies, with their distinctive uniforms, were American Red Cross volunteers who offered nonmedical services to soldiers in hospitals during the two World Wars. By the mid-1960s, uniforms for Red Cross volunteer services were no longer color-coded.

"He's a wise guy," the guard said. "Should I teach him to answer a little nicer?" He sounded eager.

"Not yet, Jack," the doctor said. "Perhaps, Mr. March, we'll let you visit Mr. Wolfe. But first I'd like to know why you want to see him. Surely you didn't come out to sell him that new policy?"

"It's one of our special services," I said.

He shook his head at me like he was reproving a child. "Let's not play childish games, Mr. March. I'm afraid you're going to be a problem, no matter what you tell me."

"You might be right," I said. "I think you and that fancy blond broad intend to turn the liability of one husband into a half-million-dollar asset. I'm here as advance notice that it won't work."

He looked at me and smiled. "But it will, Mr. March. I'm sure that no one knows you're here. Your company wouldn't dare interfere even if the old man babbled when he was there this morning. And I seriously doubt that you would go to the police with so little to go on, or that they would listen to you. Otherwise *they'd* be here instead of you dropping in over the wall. I'm afraid that your bluff won't work, Mr. March. But I will let you join Mr. Wolfe—in a fashion." He stood up and walked over to a cabinet. "I intend to give you a small amount of drug. Mr. March. You may take it in a glass of water voluntarily, or I can have Jack hold you while I give it to you by injection. Whichever you prefer."

"What is it?" I asked. "Lysergic acid diethylamide?"

He turned from the cabinet, holding a glass eyedropper and looked at me. "You are smarter than I thought," he said. "It is fortunate that we caught you as quickly as we did. Yes,

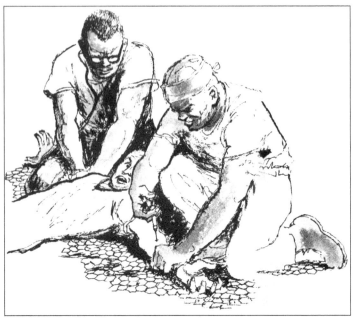

ILLUSTRATED BY HARVEY KIDDER

Mr. March, it is lysergic acid." He poured a glass of water and squeezed the eyedropper over it. "This is fifty micrograms of lysergic acid, such a small amount you can hardly see it—yet it is enough."

I felt a shiver of fear, knowing what the drug could do, but then I also knew I had an antidote for it—the chlorpromazine pills in my pocket.

"This is enough," the doctor continued, "to turn you into a schizophrenic for seven or eight hours. You know, there is one experiment that no one has yet tried; that is to keep someone continuously under the influence of the drug. Perhaps if we try it we won't have to worry about what to do with you. ... Here, drink this, Mr. March."

He handed me the glass. I took a preliminary taste. It seemed like ordinary water. I drank it down and handed him the glass. "Okay," I said. "Where's my padded cell?" I wanted to get where I could take the antidote quickly.

"There's no hurry," he said. "Go over there and sit down. I want to see how you react."

There was no point arguing. I went over and sat down on the couch, wondering what to do. I couldn't take the chlorpromazine while he was watching me, and I didn't know how long I had.

For once I didn't have any smart comeback. I sat there, silently fighting the fear within me. Schizophrenia is a form of insanity, and I expect we all have a fear of that; our modern veneer is only a very thin layer over superstition which has been with us much longer. But Herbert Wolfe had gone through what I was about to experience—several times—and I told myself that I could do it if he could.

"It is now twenty minutes since I gave you the drug," the doctor said. He was watching me intently. "You should soon start having some reactions."

I didn't feel anything except the fear and that the room wasn't quite warm enough. "Why don't you put a little heat in here?" I asked. "My feet are cold."

"That is the first symptom," he said. He glanced at his watch. "Just twenty-one minutes. Very good."

My legs were trembling slightly, but I wasn't sure whether it was from cold or fear. Dr. Borden answered it for me.

"The slight tremor in your knees," he said, "follows the coldness in the extremities."

I stared at him, realizing that I was getting angry at the way he could sit there coldly discussing what was happening to me. It seemed to amuse him. His face had taken on a long, satanical look.

"You bastard," I told him. "Instead of sitting there staring at me, why don't you go look at yourself. Then you'd really have something to laugh at."

"Emotional flatness," he said, "and distorted vision is always the next step, often accompanied by anger."

All right, I thought to myself, if he's going to treat me like a bug under a microscope, I wouldn't say another word. Not another double-damned wriggly word. I concentrated on that for a while, then I suddenly had an idea. A brilliant idea.

"I bet it's a fake," I said. "I bet there wasn't anything in that glass but water and you work on the power of suggestion. In the meantime, you and your damned guard sit around like two long-faced monkeys, with drooping jowls, and think you're so damned smart."

"Excellent," the doctor said. "General suspicion and a feeling of persecution, with continuous distortion of vision ..."

I made a suggestion about what he could do with his observations. If that was part of the symptoms, he didn't say anything. He just sat there staring at me.

Then I suddenly forgot about him.

I thought I caught a motion out of the corner of my eye. I looked around. And suddenly realized that the room was much smaller than I had thought when I first entered. Or they'd moved the walls. First I thought that was funny, then not so funny. Maybe he had the room fixed so the walls would move. Maybe he was making the room smaller, trying to frighten me. They were moving in on me. Somebody screamed—and I realized it was me.

The walls moved back into place. The scream had frightened them. I felt proud of myself.

"You are now well into the schizophrenic phase," he said. "From, here on you will experience extreme morbid feelings."

"You talk too much," I told him. "Talk, talk, talk." I was going to say more, but I noticed something. I couldn't see my hands. Just empty sleeves. But I knew I had hands. I'd had them when I came in. I tried pounding them on my knees, but I couldn't feel anything. There was a noise, all right, but Dr. Borden was probably making that, trying to fool me. I still didn't have any hands. Look, Ma, no hands. It would have been funny except that it's not funny to lose your hands. It's tragic. I felt like crying.

"Hands," I said.

"What about your hands, Mr. March?"

"Had them when I came in. You must've stolen them. Bastard. No right to take a man's hands."

I looked down, still searching for my hands, and saw the carpet on the floor undulating, the colors running together, the red and the yellow and the brown, like a herd of snakes. Are snakes a herd or a clutch? I lifted my feet away from the snakes.

There was something I had to do. Something terribly important.

"Mr. March."

Something I had to take. Important to take. But what was it?

"Mr. March."

"You don't have to shout at me,"

I said. "You're a big mouth." I didn't really care. I was watching myself float up off the couch.

I watched myself float and thought the thoughts that are unwritten and unspoken. The hidden thoughts. And somewhere Dr. Borden watched. Dr. Borden was sorden—or sordid. I giggled and the giggle turned into a scream. Everything was a four-letter obscenity. There were colors everywhere. Bright colors. Dark, angry colors. Running colors. Every room equipped with hot and cold running colors.

"Take him and lock him up," Dr. Borden said from somewhere.

A hand came out of nothing and helped me up from the couch—when had I stopped floating?—then led me away. Down a hall with walls that moved away from my touch. The hand opened a door and shoved me inside and the door closed and a lock clicked.

I fell on the floor and the floor moved like the back of a whale. I inched myself across it and pulled myself up on the bed. I fell over it, pulling away from the prying eyes. But then the eyes were gone and there was something I had to do. Milo March had to do something—everything—nothing ...

And nothing was a round ball—or an empty pill. And I remembered what I had to do. I clawed in my pockets and found the pills. I stuffed them in my mouth and looked around the room. There was a pitcher and a glass. I stumbled across the room, splashing water on the floor and into the glass. I washed the pills down and lurched back to the bed. I fell across it and waited for something to happen. I wasn't sure what. I'd forgotten.

The colors flashed and twisted against the ceiling and after a while there was nothing but a dirty white ceiling. I felt as if my whole body had been put through a giant wringer, but I was Milo March again. Then I wanted to go to sleep, but I fought it because I knew I must not.

I looked at my watch. It was almost two o'clock in the morning. I'd been at the sanatorium and under the drug for nearly four hours. There was no time to pamper myself.

I went to the door. I remembered vaguely having heard it being locked, but I tried it. It was locked, all right, and there was no keyhole on the inside. I fell against the door and began beating on it with my fists and screaming. I don't know how long I kept this up, but my fists were sore and my voice no more than a screech when I finally heard a key in the lock on the outside. I pulled back from the door, still screaming the best that I could.

The door swung open. "I'll fix you, buster," the guard was saying as he came through.

I hit him on the neck as hard as I could. The blow spun him around. I kicked then, swinging my foot to a point a few inches below his belt buckle. He grunted in pain and doubled up. As he did, I locked my hands together and brought them down hard on the back of his neck. At the same time I brought my knee up into his face. There was a crunching of cartilage and bone. He sobbed once, then his body sagged. I threw him from me and staggered out through the door.

Herbert Wolfe had to be in one of those rooms and I had to find him. I remembered the outside locks and went back to take the keys from the guard. Then I went searching again. It was the fifth door I tried. It was the only one locked. I unlocked it and looked in. Herbert Wolfe was lying curled up on the bed. His eyes were open and he was mumbling wildly to himself. And I had no more chlorpromazine. I went over and put my hand on his shoulder.

"Herbert," I said as gently as I could. "Come on. It's time to go home."

He looked up at me and giggled. "You're a long-faced baboon," he said. "Long and silly-looking."

"I'm a long-faced baboon," I said wearily, "and if we don't get out of here we'll both be swinging from the trees instead of through them." I got one arm around him and helped him to his feet. Half carrying and half dragging him, I left the room. He muttered to himself and giggled.

We went slowly down the hall and I cursed myself for not remembering to get the guard's gun. But it was too late and I was too tired to go back after it. But we were lucky. No one showed up and we made it to a door and stumbled out into the darkness. Only the dim glow from a distant streetlight threw a faint light over the wall.

Herbert stiffened in my arms. "The wall is closing in," he said. "It is dark with darkness and there are no lights. The walls are closing." He opened his mouth to scream and I clapped my hand over his lips. The scream was a whimper in his throat.

I knew I had to do something. I was too near to passing out

myself to carry him and keep him quiet. One scream from him and we'd never make it. We might not anyway. The guard wouldn't remain unconscious forever. Then I remembered the cops who were supposed to be keeping an eye on the place and prayed they weren't taking a coffee break. I fumbled in my pocket and found two packages of matches.

"Here," I said shoving one of them into Herbert's hand. "We will make more lights and then it won't be dark. Light anything that will burn." I let go of him and ran, looking for things. Once I glanced back and saw Herbert Wolfe crawling on the ground, striking matches and giggling. He wasn't doing much good, but it was keeping him occupied for the moment.

I found a barrel of trash and paper. I rolled it against the house and dropped a burning match into it. In the garage I found some oil-soaked rags. I piled them against the wood and set them afire. I carried others outside, lit them, and tossed them onto the shingle roof of the garage. I ran looking for more.

Even Herbert had finally managed to find something that would burn, for I saw two other little fires springing up. I heard his giggle turn into a whine of fear.

At least two of the fires were leaping high into the air. Then lights came on in the house and I heard someone shout. But at the same time I heard the shrill whine of a siren, and it was not far off.

It was a dead heat. The police car arrived at the front gate at the same time that Dr. Borden and another guard came out of the house with guns.

"I'm glad you arrived, officers," Dr. Borden said smoothly

as he let them in. "As you can see, these two patients some-how escaped and started these fires. Both of them are quite irrational, but I'm sure we can handle them."

Herbert Wolfe was curled up on the ground, crying.

"Nonsense," I said. "I'm not the least irrational. I'll admit I'm tired, but that's all. My name is Milo March and I'm an insurance investigator. Here's my identification. Call Lieu-tenant Dodge. He knows me and he'll tell you that I was the one who asked that a watch be kept on this place tonight."

Dr. Borden was staring at me, not understanding. I kept myself under tight control. The warring of the two drugs in my body had beaten me until it was all I could do to stand up.

"Well," one of the cops said uncertainly, "we was told to keep an eye on the place ..."

"This man is not responsible for his actions," the doctor said. "He—"

"This," I interrupted, "is Dr. Borden. I want him arrested and charged with kidnapping, assault and battery, attempted fraud and murder, and anything else you can think of. The man on the ground is Herbert Wolfe. Get him and me to the nearest hospital. Tell the doctor that we've both had lyser-gic acid but that I've had an antidote. Tell the doctor to find evidence of this. Inside the house, you'll find another guard, unconscious." I hurried the words out because I wasn't sure how much time I had.

In the distance I could hear the wail of another siren. Prob-ably the fire department.

The two policemen were still looking uncertainly at all of us. Then Dr. Borden's guard swung the scales. He started to lift his gun. One of the cops quickly stepped forward and knocked the gun from his hand. Then he swung his own gun to cover both the guard and Dr. Borden, but without losing sight of me.

"We'll take you all in," the cop said, "and then we'll get it straightened out. We'll check with the Lieutenant on the way in."

"That's what I've been saying," I said. My voice sounded like it was coming from a great distance. "Take us all in. But don't forget the hospital and the lysergic acid. And when the little guy on the ground comes around, tell him to get a new beneficiary. A homely one. I'm too tired to go through something like this again."

Then I'd had it. I knew it and I didn't even fight it any longer. I pitched forward and I felt one of the cops catch me. Then the darkness tumbled over me like a warm coat. ...

OTHER STORIES BY
KENDELL FOSTER CROSSEN—
AN ANNOTATED LIST

These are selected magazine stories, published under assorted names and pseudonyms (M.E. Chaber, Christopher Monig, Bennett Barlay, Richard Foster, and Kent Richards). Their protagonists are private eyes and insurance investigators, a playwright and a reporter, a mortician and a coroner, and even a criminal narrator. This list does not include Ken Crossen's science fiction stories; the fourteen Green Lama novellas (reissued in three volumes by Altus Press in 2011–2012); a couple of stories that appeared under the bylines Kent Richards and Bennett Barlay in Green Lama comic books of 1944 and 1946; or the Milo March stories and novellas that are listed in the foreword to this book. Note that several stories on this list are authored by M.E. Chaber, but they are not Milo March stories.

Although we are not listing science fiction, we'd like to point out the humorous Manning Draco stories of 1951–1954 (reissued in 2013 in two volumes by Altus Press) because they are about an intergalactic insurance investigator with habits reminiscent of Milo March's, except that his drink might be a green liquor shot through with amber streaks, and the shapely Martian beauty on his arm might be batting the lashes of three eyes.

1939, September 2. "The Aaron Burr Murder Case," as by Ken Crossen. *Detective Fiction Weekly.* Featuring Johnny Briggs, book reviewer for the *New York Post-Telegraph.* Crossen's very first published story.

1939, December 16. "John Brown's Body," as by Ken Crossen. *Detective Fiction Weekly.* Featuring Dick Petty, crime reporter for the *New York Globe.*

1939, December 30. "Death Is a Tourist," as by Bennett Barlay. *Detective Fiction Weekly.* Featuring Lt. Mark Nolan, Homicide, NYPD.

1940, February 3. "The Case of the Happy Undertaker," as by Bennett Barlay. *Detective Fiction Weekly.* Featuring Sgt. Stuart, Homicide, NYPD, with Mortimer Death, mortician.

1940, February 24. "One Dollar—One Corpse," as by Bennett Barlay. *Detective Fiction Weekly.* Featuring George T. Lawson, criminal.

1940, March 9, March 16, and March 23. "Satan Comes Across," as by Bennett Barlay. *Detective Fiction Weekly,* three parts. Featuring Larry Donald, novelist.

1940, March 23. "Homicide on the Hook," as by Ken Crossen. *Detective Fiction Weekly.* Featuring Paul Anthony, insurance detective. Crossen's first insurance investigator story.

1940, August 10. "The Red Rooster of Death," as by Bennett Barlay. *Detective Fiction Weekly.* Featuring Mortimer Death, mortician.

1940, October. "A Vision of Murder," as by Ken Crossen. *Stirring Detective & Western Stories.*

1940, November. "A Shield and a Club," as by Ken Crossen. *Stirring Detective & Western Stories.* Featuring Danny

O'Brian, 3rd Precinct, Cleveland Police Dept.

1940, December 14. "The Cat and the Foil," as by Ken Crossen. *Detective Fiction Weekly*. Featuring Johnny "Mad" Hatter, insurance detective with Great Northern Insurance Co.

1941, January 25. "The Bowman of Mons," as by Ken Crossen. *Argosy*.

1941, April 12. "Prest-O Change-O Murder," as by Bennett Barlay. *Detective Fiction Weekly*. Featuring Mortimer Death, mortician.

1941, April 19. "The Ears of Loretta," as by Ken Crossen. *Detective Fiction Weekly*. Featuring Johnny "Mad" Hatter, insurance detective with Great Northern Insurance Co.

1941, April 26. "Fifty to One Is Murder," as by Bennett Barlay. *Detective Fiction Weekly*. Featuring Borden Cheever, private detective.

1941, May 17. "The Miniature Murders," as by Ken Crossen. *Detective Fiction Weekly*. Featuring Johnny "Mad" Hatter, insurance detective with Great Northern Insurance Co.

1941, May 31. "The Crime in the Wastebasket," as by Bennett Barlay. *Detective Fiction Weekly*. A locked-room mystery featuring Lt. Valentine Varritt, Office of Odd Complaints, NYPD.

1941, June. "Three on a Murder," as by Kent Richards. *Double Detective*. Featuring Barry Crantan, private detective.

1941, June 21. "Axe for the Parson," as by Ken Crossen. *Detective Fiction Weekly*. Featuring Dick Petty, crime reporter, and Rev. Eben Chesser, "The Parson."

1941, June 14. "Too Late for Murder," as by Bennett Barlay.

Detective Fiction Weekly. Featuring Mortimer Death, mortician.

1941, July 12. "Murder as a Fine Art," as by Ken Crossen. *Detective Fiction Weekly.* Featuring Lt. Dale Mann, NYPD; Prof. Anton Stagg; and Dr. Jonah Forrest, coroner.

1941, July 19. "Trouble with Twins," as by Ken Crossen. *Detective Fiction Weekly.* Featuring Johnny "Mad" Hatter, insurance detective with Great Northern Insurance Co.

1941, August 2. "And So to Murder," as by Ken Crossen. *Detective Fiction Weekly.* Featuring Lt. Dale Mann, NYPD; Prof. Anton Stagg; and Dr. Jonah Forrest, coroner.

1941, November 15. "Murder Wins an Oscar," as by Kent Richards. *Detective Fiction Weekly.* Featuring Barry Crantan, private detective.

1941, December. "My Kid Brother—A Killer?" as by Ken Crossen. *All Star Detective.*

1942, March. "The Laughing Killer," as by Bennett Barlay. *Keyhole Detective Cases.*

1942, March. "Love on the Panhandle," as by Richard Foster. *Keyhole Detective Cases.*

1942, March. "Satan's Mistress," as by Kent Richards. *Keyhole Detective Cases.*

1943, January. "The Laughing Buddha Murders," as by Ken Crossen. *Flynn's Detective Fiction.* A locked-room mystery featuring Chin Kwang Kham, Tibetan private eye in New York City. Reissued in 1944 in paperback, as by Richard Foster. A sequel to this novella was published as a paperback original, *The Invisible Man Murders* (Five Star Mystery #5, 1945), as by Richard Foster.

1943, March. "All Dressed Up," as by Richard Foster. *Baffling Detective Mysteries.*

1943, March. "Blonde Trouble," as by Kent Richards. *Baffling Detective Mysteries.*

1943, March. "Murder Goes Overboard," as by Richard Foster. *Baffling Detective Mysteries.*

1943, May. "An Angle to Murder," as by Bennett Barlay. *Baffling Detective Mysteries.*

1943, May. "The Case of the Curious Heel," as by Ken Crossen. *Baffling Detective Mysteries.* A locked-room mystery. Also published as paperbacks: William H. Wise (an Eerie Series Publication), 1942, and Eerie Series, 1944.

1943, May. "Death's Key Ring," as by Richard Foster. *Baffling Detective Mysteries.*

1943, July. "A Killer's Number," as by Richard Foster. *Baffling Detective Mysteries.*

1944, March 22. "The Parsons Returns," as by Ken Crossen. *Detective Fiction Weekly.* Featuring Dick Petty, crime reporter, and Rev. Eben Chesser, "The Parson." Sequel to "Axe for the Parson" (1941).

1945, March. "The Crime in the Envelope," as by Bennett Barlay. *Banner Mysteries* (vol. 1, no. 1), edited by Ken Crossen. "The world's smallest locked-room mystery," featuring Lt. Valentine Varritt, Bureau of Odd Complaints, NYPD. Bibliographer Phil Stephenson-Payne writes of *Banner Mysteries:* "While usually regarded as a book series, some authorities consider this a magazine because of the presence of a second story, by a different author, in the first 'issue.' " The second story in this issue was "The Sunday

Pigeon Murders" by Craig Rice. "The Crime in the Envelope" was reprinted as by Ken Crossen in the anthology *Murder Cavalcade,* edited by Ken Crossen (Duell, Sloan, and Pierce, 1946).*

1945, March. "A Long Time Dead," as by Ken Crossen. *New Detective Magazine.*

1952, November. "Anything for a Thrill," as by M.E. Chaber. *Popular Detective.* Cover line: "Teenagers on the loose!"

1952, December. "Death Bait," as by Kendell Foster Crossen. *Mobsters: Stories of the Fight against the Underworld.* Cover line: "She learned her power over men too young." Basis for the novel *The Girl from Easy Street* (1955), as by Richard Foster.

1953, February. "The Death Makers," as by M.E. Chaber. *Mobsters: Stories of the Fight against the Underworld.* Cover line: "A novel of tough men—and women."

1953, November. "Renegade!" as by M.E. Chaber. *Sea Stories.*

1953, December. "The Red Candle," as by Christopher Monig. *Bluebook* (A Bluebook Novelette). Espionage adventure featuring Maj. Kim Locke, U.S. Army, and his dog, Dante.

1953, Winter. "The White Death," as by Richard Foster. A Dan Fowler novel. *G-Men Detective.*

1954, January. "Murder on the Inside," as by M.E. Chaber. Featuring Lt. Shaun Bradley. *Bluebook.* Prison mayhem.

1954, Winter. "Precinct 23," as by M.E. Chaber. *Triple Detective.*

1955. "The Murder Tap," as by Kendell Foster Crossen.

---

* *Murder Cavalcade* was the first of the Mystery Writers of America anthologies. Most sources give the editor simply as the MWA, but a historical survey on the MWA website confirms that Ken Crossen was the editor.

Stories Annual. Featuring private eye Harry Hamal. This was the first issue of this annual collection of sci-fi, western, and crime stories. The story title is often misprinted as "The Murder Trap."

1955, October. "The Treatment," as by Kendell Foster Crossen. *Stag Magazine.* Adapted from chapter 4 of *The Tortured Path* (1957), an espionage novel as by Kendell Foster Crossen, featuring Maj. Kim Locke undergoing brainwashing in Red China. The prisoner in the story, who is held in solitary to the point of madness, is not identified as Locke.

1957, January. "Hungry Doll," as by M.E. Chaber. *Adventure Trails.*

1957, February. "Call Girl Bait," as by Kendell Foster Crossen. *Male.*

ABOUT THE AUTHOR

Kendell Foster Crossen (1910–1981), the only child of Samuel Richard Crossen and Clo Foster Crossen, was born on a farm outside Albany in Athens County, Ohio—a village of some 550 souls in the year of this birth. His ancestors on his mother's side include the 19th-century songwriter Stephen Collins Foster ("Oh! Susanna"); William  Allen, founder of Allentown, Pennsylvania; and Ebenezer Foster, one of the Minute Men who sprang to arms at the Lexington alarm in April 1775.

Ken went to Rio Grande College on a football scholarship but stayed only one year. "When I was fairly young, I developed the disgusting habit of reading," says Milo March, and it seems Ken Crossen, too, preferred self-education. He loved literature and poetry; favorite authors included Christopher Marlowe and Robert Service. He also enjoyed participant sports and was a semi-pro fighter in the heavyweight class. He became a practicing magician and had a passion for chess.

After college Ken wrote several one-act plays that were produced in a small Cleveland theater. He worked in steel mills and Fisher Body plants. Then he was employed as an insurance investigator, or "claims adjuster," in Cleveland. But he left the job and returned to the theater, now as a performer: a tumbling clown in the Tom Mix Circus; a comic and carnival barker for a tent show, and an actor in a medicine show.

In 1935, Ken hitchhiked to New York City with a typewriter under his arm, and found work with the WPA Writers' Project, covering cricket for the *New York City Guidebook.* In 1936, he was hired by the Munsey Publishing Company as associate editor of the popular *Detective Fiction Weekly.* The company asked him to come up with a character to compete with The Shadow, and thus was born a unique superhero of pulps, comic books, and radio—The Green Lama, an American mystic trained in Tibetan Buddhism.

Crossen sold his first story, "The Aaron Burr Murder Case," to *Detective Fiction Weekly* in September 1939, but says he didn't begin to make a living from writing till 1941. He tried his hand at publishing true crime magazines, comics, and a picture magazine, without great success, so he set out for Hollywood. From his typewriter flowed hundreds of stories, short novels for magazines, scripts radio, television, and film, nonfiction articles. He delved into science fiction in the 1950s, starting with "Restricted Clientele" (February 1951). His dystopian novels *Year of Consent* and *The Rest Must Die* also appeared in this decade.

In the course of his career Ken Crossen acquired six pseudonyms: Richard Foster, Bennett Barlay, Kent Richards, Clay
Richards, Christopher Monig, and M.E. Chaber. The variety
was necessary because different publishers wanted to reserve
specific bylines for their own publications. Ken based "M.E.
Chaber" on the Hebrew word for "author," *mechaber.*

In the early '50s, as M.E. Chaber, Crossen began to write
a series of full-length mystery/espionage novels featuring
Milo March, an insurance investigator. The first, *Hangman's
Harvest,* was published in 1952. In all, there are twenty-two
Milo March novels. One, *The Man Inside,* was made into a
British film starring Jack Palance.

Most of Ken's characters were private detectives, and Milo
was the most popular. Paperback Library reissued twenty-five
Crossen titles in 1970–1971, with covers by Robert McGinnis. Twenty were Milo March novels, four featured an insurance investigator named Brian Brett, and one was about CIA
agent Kim Locke.

Crossen excelled at producing well-plotted entertainment
with fast-moving action. His research skills were a strong
asset, back when research meant long hours searching library
microfilms and poring over street maps and hotel floorplans.
His imagination took him to many international hot spots,
although he himself never traveled abroad. Like Milo March,
he hated flying ("When you've seen one cloud, you've seen
them all").

Ken Crossen was married four times. With his first wife he
had three children (Stephen, Karen, Kendra) and with his
second a son (David). He lived in New York, Florida, South-

ern California, Nevada, and other parts of the country. Milo March moves from Denver to New York City after five books of the series, with an apartment on Perry Street in Greenwich Village; that's where Ken lived, too. His and Milo's favorite watering hole was the Blue Mill Tavern, a short walk from the apartment.

Ken Crossen was a combination of many of the traits of his different male characters: tough, adventuresome, with a taste for gin and shapely women. But perhaps the best observation was made in an obituary written by sci-fi writer Avram Davidson, who described Ken as a fundamentally gentle person who had been buffeted by many winds.

CPSIA information can be obtained
at www.ICGtesting.com
Printed in the USA
BVHW031324170621
609832BV00006B/27